A Bridge to the Other Side:

Death in the Folk Tradition

A Bridge to the Other Side:

Death in the Folk Tradition

Michael Berman

MOON
BOOKS

Winchester, UK
Washington, USA

First published by Moon Books, 2012
Moon Books is an imprint of John Hunt Publishing Ltd., Laurel House, Station Approach,
Alresford, Hants, SO24 9JH, UK
office1@o-books.net
www.o-books.com

For distributor details and how to order please visit the 'Ordering' section on our website.

Text copyright: Michael Berman 2011

ISBN: 978 1 78099 256 3

A CIP catalogue record for this book is available from the British Library.

Design: Stuart Davies

Printed and bound by CPI Group (UK) Ltd, Croydon, CR0 4YY
Printed in the USA by Offset Paperback Mfrs, Inc

We operate a distinctive and ethical publishing philosophy in all
areas of our business, from our global network of authors to
production and worldwide distribution.

CONTENTS

Acknowledgement

It was with great sadness that I read of the death of John Bruno Hare this year. He was the founder of the Internet Sacred Text Archive, (http://www.sacred-texts.com), an invaluable source of material that I have made use of for this book and others that I have written.

He died of cancer on April 27, 2010, but was apparently busy transcribing religious texts and finding inspiration from them right up to the end of his life (http://twitter.com/sacredtexts),

His death will be a great loss to researchers working in the field of religious studies worldwide.

MB, 2011

Introduction

We must all die; we are like water spilled on the ground,
which cannot be gathered up
2 Samuel 14:14

A Bridge to the Other Side is a collection of articles and traditional folk tales that deal with our feelings about and attitudes towards Death, both our own death and that of those nearest and dearest to us. The study of how ancient peoples understood and responded to death can add to our own understanding and self-development, and this is what led to the writing of this book.

A bridge between earth and heaven, this world and the next, features in the mythology of many different peoples. For example, in Norse legends, Bifröst or Bilröst is a burning rainbow bridge between Midgard, the world, and Asgard, the realm of the gods. The bridge is known as *Bilröst* in the *Poetic Edda*; compiled in the 13th century from earlier traditional sources, and as *Bifröst* in the *Prose Edda*; written in the 13th century by Snorri Stureuson. Both the *Poetic Edda* and the *Prose Edda* alternately refer to the bridge as Asbrú (Old Norse Æsirs' "bridge"). The Persians believed in a bridge between earth and paradise too. In his prayers the penitent in his confession would say: "I am wholly without doubt in the existence of the Mazdayaçnian faith; in the coming of the resurrection of the latter body; in the stepping *over the bridge Chinvat*; as well as in the continuance of paradise."

Over the midst of the Moslem hell stretches the bridge Es-Sirat, "finer than a hair and sharper than the edge of a sword." In the Lyke-Wake Dirge of the English north-country, they sang of "The Brig of Dread, Na braider than a thread." In Borneo the passage for souls to heaven is across a long tree; it is scarcely practicable to any except those who have killed a man. In Burma, among the Karens, they tie strings across the rivers, for the ghosts of the dead to pass over to their graves. In Java, a bridge leads across the abyss to the dwelling-place of the gods; the evil-doers fall into the depths *below*. Among the Esquimaux the soul crosses an awful gulf over a stretched rope, until it reaches the abode of "the great female evil spirit below the sea." The Ojibways cross to paradise on a great snake, which serves as a bridge. The Choctaw bridge is a slippery pine-log. The South American Manacicas cross on a wooden bridge. Among many of the American tribes, the Milky Way is the bridge to the other world.

... The Slavs believed in a pathway or road which led to the other world; it was both the rainbow (as in the Gothic legends) and the Milky Way; and, since the journey was long, they put boots into the coffin, (for it was made on foot,) and coins to pay the ferrying across a wide sea, even as the Greeks expected to be carried over the Styx by Charon. This abode of the dead, at the end of this long pathway, was *an island*, a warm, fertile land, called *Buyau*. And in their effort to restore the dead men to the happy island-home, the heavenly land, beyond the water, the Norsemen actually set their dead heroes afloat in boats on the open ocean (Taken from *Ragnarok: The Age of Fire and Gravel*, by Ignatius Donnelly [1883]. Pp. 386-387 {scanned at sacred-texts.com, December, 2001}).

What can be seen from this is that the euphemistic idiom to "cross over" is an apt one, and it also explains what led me to choose the title for this book.

Where the Secret Lies

Asking which direction to take serves no purpose
There is only one, the one towards your death,
And what matters is what you do on that path
Whose lives you touch in a beneficial way
And the way you spend the time you have been blessed with
In other words, how you prepare for the only destiny that
    knowingly awaits you
As to how you can make the most of the time you have left—
Paradoxically by leaving this reality more often than you do
And by spending more of it with your true teacher and helpers
Where there are no distorting mirrors and you can receive the
    truth direct
Not channelled into the words you would rather hear
And that would enable you to justify carrying on as you are
Instead of bringing about the changes that are needed.

Death - the Partner that Waits for All of Us

"Living with the immediacy of death helps you sort out your priorities in life.
It helps you to live a less trivial life."
Sogyal Rinpoche.

In an age when keeping death at bay seems to have become an obsession for many of us, judging by the array of anti-ageing products and treatment now available on the market, a story about someone who chooses to embrace it comes as something of a surprise. Yet there are those for whom it may well appear to be the most attractive option:

Death the Sweetheart

There was once a pretty young girl with no husband, no father, no mother, and no brothers. In fact, no family at all: they were all dead and gone. She lived alone in a hut at the end of the village; and no one came near her, and she never went near anyone either. She kept herself to herself. One evening a goodly wanderer came to her, opened the door, and cried, 'I'm a wanderer, and I've travelled far in this world. Here will I rest; I can no further go.' The maiden said, 'Stay here then. I will give you a mattress to sleep on, and, if you like, something to eat and drink too.' The goodly wanderer soon lay down and said, 'Now once again I sleep; it's so long since I slept last:' 'How long?' asked the girl; and he answered, 'Dear maid, I sleep but one week in a thousand years.' The girl laughed and said, 'You're joking, surely?' But the wanderer was already fast asleep and did not answer.

Early next morning he arose and this is what he said to her. 'You're a pretty young girl and, if it pleases you, I'll stay here a whole week longer.' She gladly agreed, for already she loved the goodly wanderer. So once they were sleeping, and she roused him and said, 'Dear man, I dreamt such an evil dream. I dreamt you'd grown cold and white, and we drove in a beautiful carriage, drawn by six white birds. You blew on a mighty horn; then dead folk came up and went with us—you were their king.' Then, answered the goodly wanderer, 'That was an evil dream.' Straightway he got up and said, 'Beloved, I must go, for not a soul has died this long while in the whole world. I must be off, let me go.' But the girl wept. 'Don't go away; stay with me.' 'I must go,' he answered, 'God keep you.' But, as he gave her his hand, she said sobbing, 'Tell me, dear man, who are you then' 'Who knows that dies,' said the wanderer, 'so you ask in vain; I don't dare tell you who I am.' Then the girl wept and said, 'I don't care what happens to me and I'm prepared for anything, only do tell me who you are, please. Do me this one last favour.' 'Good,' said the man,' 'then you come with me because I'm Death.' And nobody ever saw or heard of her again.

Adapted from a Transylvanian-Roma story in Groome, F.H. (1899) *Gypsy Folk Tales*, London: Hurst & Blackett. Scanned, proofed and formatted at sacred-texts.com, December 2005, by John Bruno Hare. This text is in the public domain in the United States because it was published prior to 1923, and in the EU and other 'death+70' countries because the author died in 1902.

Also known as 'Gypsies', the Roma are nomads who originated in India during the middle ages, and spread across a wide section of Eurasia, preserving a unique culture and language. The term Gypsy was applied to the Roma by outsiders, possibly in the mistaken belief that they were Egyptian in origin. Some people today take it to be pejorative, and at the very least its use is deprecated. Nevertheless, it is used widely in the literature, particularly in books now in the public domain, by scholars who cannot be construed as using it in a derogative sense.

It is interesting to compare and contrast the Roma story with the lyrics of the traditional English folksong entitled "Death and the Lady", a version of which is presented below. For even though the lady in the song puts up a fight instead of succumbing willingly, her fate remains the same, as it does of course for all of us. The song was collected in 1946 by Francis M. Collison from Mr Baker of Maidstone, Kent, and published in Ralph Vaughan Williams and A.L. Lloyd's *Penguin Book of English Folk Songs:*

Death and the Lady

As I walked out one morn in May,
The birds did sing and the lambs did play,
The birds did sing and the lambs did play,
I met an old man,
I met an old man by the way.

His head was bald, his beard was grey,
His coat was of a myrtle shade,
I asked him what strange countryman,
Or what strange place,
Or what strange place he did belong.

"My name is Death, cannot you see?
Lords, dukes and ladies bow down to me.
And you are one of those branches three,
And you fair maid,
And you fair maid must come with me."

"I'll give you gold and jewels rare,
I'll give you costly robes to wear,
I'll give you all my wealth in store,
If you'll let me live,
If you'll let me live a few years more."

"Fair lady, lay your robes aside,
No longer glory in your pride.
And now, sweet maid, make no delay,
Your time is come,
Your time is come and you must away."

And not long after this fair maid died;
"Write on my tomb," the lady cried,
"Here lies a poor distressed maid,
Whom Death now lately,
Whom Death now lately hath betrayed."

A Sense of Humour Helps!

A man goes into a doctor's surgery. The doctor says, "Oh, Mr. Jones! We have the results of your test. Do you want the bad news first or the very bad news?"

The man shrugs and says, "Well I guess I'll have the bad news first."

"Well the bad news is, you have 24 hours to live," the doctor replies.

The man is distraught, "24 hours to live? That's horrible! What could be worse than that? What's the VERY bad news?"

The doctor folds his hands and sighs, "The very bad news is...I've been trying to contact you to tell you since yesterday."

Heaven and Hell

One day while walking down the street a highly successful HR Manager was tragically hit by a bus and she died. Her soul arrived up in heaven where she was met at the Pearly Gates by St. Peter himself.

"Welcome to Heaven," said St. Peter. "Before you get settled in though, it seems we have a problem. You see, strangely enough, we've never once had a Human Resources Manager make it this far and we're not really sure what to do with you."

"No problem, just let me in," said the woman. "Well, I'd like to," replied St. Peter, "but I have higher orders. What we're going to do is let you have a day in Hell and a day in Heaven and then you can choose whichever one you want to spend an eternity in."

"Actually, I think I've made up my mind, I prefer to stay in Heaven," said the woman.

"Sorry, but we have rules and we have to follow them." And with that St. Peter put the executive in a lift and it went down-down-down to hell. The doors opened and she found herself stepping out onto the putting green of a beautiful golf course. In the distance was a country club and standing in front of her were all her friends—fellow executives that she had worked with, and they were all dressed in evening gowns and cheering for her. They ran up and kissed her on both cheeks and they talked about old times. They played an excellent round of golf and at night went to the country club where she enjoyed an excellent steak and lobster dinner. She met the Devil who was actually quite a nice bloke and she had a great time telling jokes and dancing. She was having such a good time that before she knew it, it was time to leave. Everybody shook her hand and waved good-bye as she got into the lift. The lift went up-up-up and opened back up at the Pearly Gates and she found St. Peter waiting for her.

"Now it's time to spend a day in heaven," he said. So she

spent the next 24 hours lounging around on clouds and playing the harp and singing. She had a great time and before she knew it her 24 hours were up and St. Peter came and got her. "So, you've spent a day in hell and you've spent a day in heaven. Now you must choose your eternity," he said. The woman paused for a second and then replied, "Well, I never thought I'd say this, I mean, Heaven has been really great and all, but I think I had a better time in Hell." So St. Peter escorted her to the lift and again she went down-down-down back to Hell.

When the doors of the elevator opened she found herself standing in a desolate wasteland covered in rubbish and filth. She saw her friends were dressed in rags and were picking up the rubbish and putting it in sacks. The Devil came up to her and put his arm around her.

"I don't understand," stammered the woman, "yesterday I was here and there was a golf course and a country club and we ate lobster and we danced and had a great time. Now all there is, is a wasteland of rubbish and all my friends look miserable."

The Devil looked at her and smiled. "Yesterday we were recruiting you, today you're staff..."

The Art of Necromancy

Necromancy is a form of magic in which the practitioner seeks to summon the spirit of a deceased person, either as an apparition or ghost, or to raise them bodily, for the purpose of divination. Early necromancers, like shamans, called upon spirits such as the ghosts of ancestors. And according to Luck (2006), the way they addressed the dead, in "a mixture of high-pitch squeaking and low droning", bore similarities to the trance-state mutterings of shamans too.

The oldest literary account of necromancy is in Homer's Odyssey, from around 700 BC (see Golden, 2006, p.808). Odysseus under the tutelage of Circe, a powerful sorceress, journeys to Hades, the Underworld, in an effort to raise the spirits of the dead using spells he learnt from her. His intention is to invoke and ask questions of the shade of Tiresias, to gain insight into the impending voyage home. He discovers, however, he is unable to summon the spirit without the assistance of others. In Homer's passage, there are many references to specific rituals associated with necromancy; the rites must be done at night and around a pit with fire. In addition, Odysseus has to follow a specific recipe, which included using sacrificial animals' blood for ghosts to drink, while he recites prayers to both the ghosts and gods of the underworld. In Greek Mythology the dead are referred to as living in the underworld, and the main form of necromancy involves heroes travelling to Hades and claiming souls.

Rituals in necromancy involved magic circles, wands, talismans, bells, and incantations (see Guiley, 2006, p.215). Also, the necromancer would surround himself with morbid aspects of death, which often included wearing the deceased's clothing, consumption of unsalted, unleavened black bread and unfermented grape juice, which symbolised decay and lifelessness (ibid p.215). Necromancers even went as far as taking part in the mutilation and consumption of corpses (ibid p. 215). Rituals such as these could carry on for hours, days, even weeks leading up the summoning of spirits, and often took place in graveyards. Additionally, necromancers preferred summoning the recently departed, citing that their revelations were spoken more clearly; this timeframe usually consisted of 12 months following the death of the body (Lewis, 1999, p.201). Once this time period lapsed, necromancers would summon the deceased's ghostly spirit to appear instead.

There are also many references to necromancers, called "bone-conjurers", in the Bible. The Book of Deuteronomy (XVIII 9–12) explicitly warns the Israelites against the Canaanite practice of divination from the dead:

When thou art come into the land which the LORD thy God giveth thee, thou shalt not learn to do according to the abominations of those nations. There shall not be found among you any one who maketh his son or his daughter to pass through the fire, or who useth divination, or an observer of times, or an enchanter, or a witch, or a charmer, or a consulter with familiar spirits, or a wizard, or a necromancer. For all who do these things are an abomination unto the LORD, and because of these abominations the LORD thy God doth drive them out from before thee (KJV).

This warning was not always heeded though: King Saul had the Witch of Endor invoke the shade of Samuel, from Sheol, using a magical amulet, for example.

The Witch of Endor called up the ghost of the prophet Samuel, at the demand of King Saul in the First Book of Samuel, chapter 28:3–25. After Samuel's death and burial with due mourning ceremonies, Saul had driven out all necromancers and magicians from Israel. But then, in a bitter irony, after he received no answer from God as to his best course of action against the assembled forces of the Philistines, anonymously and in disguise, Saul sought out the witch. Following the orders of the king, the woman summons the ghost of Samuel, to give Saul advice, but he is disappointed. For after complaining of being woken up from his long sleep, the prophet's ghost berates Saul for disobeying God, and predicts his downfall, together with his whole army, in battle the next day, and adds that Saul and his sons will then join him in the abode of the dead. The next day the army is defeated and Saul commits suicide after being wounded

We know that necromancy, or the consultation of the dead, was widespread among ancient Near Eastern people, and in the Old Testament it is referred to several times: in several Pentateuchal prohibitions; in the infamous story of Saul at Endor mentioned above (the only narrative account); in the summary of Manasseh's sin and of Josiah's reform, and twice in Isiah (see Johnston, 2002, p.150). Many scholars suggest that necromancy was more widespread in Israel than the Old Testament record indicates to be the case, until the great reforms first of Hezekiah in the eighth century and then particularly of Josiah in the seventh. Until then Israelite religion was much less uniform than the Old Testament implies, and included many practices which were later to be rejected (ibid p.153).

The Hebrew word 'ôb can be translated as medium, ghost, or 'ventriloquist (engastrimuthos), and the Talmud states that mediums hid air bags in their armpits to produce a hissing sound which was then attributed to the dead' (Johnston, 2002, p.161). This suggests that a demonstrative ritual of a séance was often performed by practitioners of the art.

The Talmud, a central text for mainstream Judaism, makes mention of two kinds of necromancy, one in which the dead was raised by naming him, the other in which he was questioned by means of a skull. It is unlikely, however, that they were still employed by the Middle Ages as the references to them do not carry conviction. Other methods seem to have been more popular, such as the practice of two friends covenanting that the first to die would return to reveal the secrets of the celestial realm to the other. He might do so in a dream, but he could also appear during waking hours. Other methods described in the sources included:

1. "incantations" at the grave, which were apparently not favoured, for the word *lahash* usually denotes a forbidden type of magic; 2. spending the night on the grave, clothed in a distinctive garment and burning spices and incense while waving a myrtle wand, "until one hears an exceedingly faint voice from the grave responding to his questions, so faint that it seems hardly to be sensed by the ear, but rather to exist in his thoughts"; this method was also frowned upon for it was included in the forbidden category of magic which depends solely upon "the performance of an act" for its results; 3. "A man and a woman station themselves at the head and foot of a grave, and on the earth between them they set a rattle, which they strike while they recite a secret invocation; then while the woman looks on the man puts the questions, and the deceased reveals the future to them"; 4. a method which seems to have been acceptable, for it invoked the dead by means of angelic names: "Stand before the grave and recite the names of the angels of the fifth camp of the first firmament, and hold in your hand a mixture of oil and honey in a new glass bowl, and say, 'I conjure you, spirit of the grave, NeAinah, who rests in the grave upon the bones of the dead, that you accept this offering from my hand and do my bidding; bring me N son of N who is dead, and make him stand erect and speak with me without fear, and have him tell me the truth without fear, and I shall not be afraid of him; let him answer the question which I shall put to him'; and the deceased will immediately appear. But if he doesn't, repeat this invocation a second time, and if necessary, a third. When he appears place the bowl before him, and converse with him. Hold a myrtle wand in your hand." [Myrtle, hazel and hawthorn are the types of wood

favoured in magic, and most often prescribed for the indispensable magician's staff, the divining-rod, the witch's broomstick, etc.]. (Trachtenberg, 1939, Chapter XIV)

Although Israelite life and faith were centred on the present life and relating to Yahweh in the here and now, and Death was regarded very much as the end of this life, rather than the start of the next as was the case among other ancient Near Eastern peoples (see Johnston, 2002, p.65), we are offered some hope of an afterlife. For we learn that one day Yahweh will truly deliver his people. Those who sleep in the dust of the earth will awake, some to everlasting life, and some to shame and contempt (see Dan. 12:2). We are also told that the dead shall live and sing for joy once more (see Is. 26:19). But no further details are provided.

Norse mythology also contains examples of necromancy (Ruickbie, 2004, p.48), such as the scene in the *Völuspá* in which Odin summons a seeress from the dead to tell him of the future. In Grógaldr, the first part of Svipdagsmál, the hero Svipdag summons his dead Völva mother, Gróa, to cast spells for him. In *Hrólf Kraki's saga*, the half-elven princess Skuld was very skilled in witchcraft (seiðr), and this to the point that she was almost invincible in battle. When her warriors fell, she made them rise again to continue fighting.

Many medieval writers believed resurrection was impossible without the assistance of the Christian God. They translated the practice of divination as conjuring demons who took the appearance of spirits. The practice became known explicitly as demonic magic and was condemned by the Roman Catholic Church.

References

Guiley, R. E. (2006) *The Encyclopedia of Magic and Alchemy*, New York: Facts on File.

Johnston, P.S. (2002) *Shades of Sheol: Death and Afterlife in the Old*

Testament, Downers Grove, Illinois: InterVarsity Press.

Luck, G. (2006). *Arcana Mundi: Magic and the Occult in the Greek and Roman Worlds* (Second Edition). The Johns Hopkins University Press: Baltimore.

Golden, R. M. (ed.) (2006) *Encyclopedia of Witchcraft the Western Tradition*, California: ABC-CLIO.

Ruickbie, L. (2004) *Witchcraft Out of the Shadows*, London: Robert Hale.

Trachtenberg, J. (1939) *Jewish Magic and Superstition: A Study in Folk Religion*, New York: Behrman's Jewish Book House.

Like an Ocean is this World

The following poem, by Hovhannes Erzingatzi (b: 1260), is taken from Boyajian's 1916 collection entitled *Armenian Legends and Poems*

LIKE an ocean is this world;
None undrenched may cross that ocean.
My ship too its sails unfurled,
Ere I knew it was in motion.

Now we draw towards the land,
And I fear the sea-board yonder: —
Lest the rocks upon the strand
Break and tear our planks asunder.

I will pray God that He raise
From the shore a breeze to meet us,
To disperse this gloomy haze,
That a happy land may greet us.

Reference

Boyajian, Z.C. (compiler) (1916) *Armenian Legends and Poems*, London, J. M. Dent & Sons Ltd. Scanned at sacred-texts.com, June 2006. Proofed and formatted by John Bruno Hare. This text is in the public domain in the USA and the files may be used for any non-commercial purpose, provided this notice of attribution is left intact in all copies.

The Bride in her Grave

Rabbi Yisroel (Israel) ben Eliezer (1698-1760), often called Baal Shem Tov or Besht, was a Jewish mystical rabbi and is regarded by many to be the founder of Hasidic Judaism. The title *Baal Shem Tov* is usually translated into English as "Master of the Good Name", although it is more correctly understood as a combination of *Baal Shem* ("Master of the [Divine] Name") and *Tov* (an honorific epithet to the man).

The little biographical information that is known about Besht is so interwoven with legends of miracles that in many cases it is hard to arrive at the historical facts. From the numerous stories connected with his birth it appears that his parents were poor, upright, and pious. When he was orphaned, his community cared for him. At school, he distinguished himself only by his frequent disappearances, being always found in the lonely woods surrounding the place, rapturously enjoying the beauties of nature. What follows is one of the many supposedly true stories about his exploits.

* * *

In time the whole world grew to know of the wisdom and power of the Baal Shem Tov, and from all corners of the Carpathians, followers came to him. Often he went on journeys to far places to which the Will had called him.

Once on a Wednesday night Rabbi Israel arose and said, "I must go away for the Sabbath." He went into the barn and harnessed his horse.

Several of his followers sprang after him and begged that he take them with him. But he allowed only a few of them to come into his wagon.

"Where will we hold Sabbath?" they said.

"In Berlin, in the house of a wealthy Jew."

Though they knew that with swiftest horses it took more than a week to reach Berlin, they did not question the Rabbi, for the Master was not confined in the bonds of time or of space.

The Baal Shem let his little horse walk slowly along a byway all that evening, and at midnight the wagon stopped before a tavern.

"Let us stay here tonight," said Rabbi Israel.

The tavern-keeper welcomed them into his house, for he saw that they were holy men.

"Perhaps you will honour my house, and remain over Sabbath?" he said.

But Rabbi Israel answered, "We must hold Sabbath in Berlin."

The inn-keeper looked at him, and did not understand. The Rabbi said, "On Sabbath eve there is to be a wedding in the house of a wealthy Jew of Berlin, and I must be at the wedding in order to read the service, and bless the bride."

"You must have a wonderful horse," said the tavern-keeper, smiling.

"My little horse will get me there in time," said Rabbi Israel.

"In time for the Sabbath after this one," answered the inn-keeper, laughing. "Why, Berlin is farther than a hundred miles away. If you were to travel day and night, sparing neither man nor beast, you might arrive in time for the Sabbath after this one."

But his words did not trouble the Baal Shem Tov. Rabbi Israel turned to his followers and said, "You are tired. Let us go to sleep."

The tavern-keeper could not sleep that night. He lay awake wondering how the Rabbi would reach Berlin before the Sabbath fell. "This is Wednesday night," he said.

"Tomorrow is a day, and Friday is only part of a day. No, I cannot understand it!" At last he said to himself, "I will tell him I have things to attend to in Berlin, and ask him to take me there."

When the Baal Shem Tov arose in the morning, the tavern-keeper ran to him saying, "Shall I harness the horse, Rabbi?"

"Not yet," said the Baal Shem Tov. "First we will pray. And after that, we will eat our breakfast."

"Rabbi," said the inn-keeper, "I have business to do in Berlin. Take me there with you!"

"When we start, come with us in our wagon," said Rabbi Israel.

The Master and his followers said the morning prayers, and after that they sat down around the table. They ate without haste, and while they ate they discussed the Torah.

A problem of judgement arose, and they sat a long time discussing the problem.

Meanwhile the inn-keeper ran and dressed himself for the journey. When he was ready, he looked into the room where the Master sat with his students, and he saw them still absorbed in their discussions.

"Half the day is gone already!" thought the inn-keeper.

He heard Rabbi Israel's words. "Of every good deed we do, a good angel is born. Of every bad deed, a bad angel is born. In all the deeds of our daily life we serve God as directly as though our deeds were prayers. When we eat, when we work, when we sing, when we wash ourselves, we are praying to God.

"Therefore we should live constantly in highest joy, for everything that we do is an offer to God.

"And of those things that we do badly, work that we leave half finished, or thoughts that we leave uncompleted, malformed angels are born. Angels without heads, angels with no eyes, angels without arms, without hair, without feet. Therefore no deed should be left unfinished."

The inn-keeper thought, "If that is the way he travels to Berlin, the angel born of his ride will have perhaps the beginning of a toe, and nothing else."

But the rabbi and his students remained around the table, talking.

"I will tell you the story of a king," said the Baal Shem Tov. "There was a very wise king who had built for himself a strange and wonderful palace. In the centre of the palace was a room in which stood the throne. Only one door led into this room. All through the palace were passageways and halls and corridors that turned and twisted about and led in every direction, there were endless walls without openings, and there were more corridors and more passageways.

"When the palace stood finished, the King sent an order to all of his lords commanding them to come before him. He sat on his throne and waited.

"The lords came to the outside of the Palace, and stared in wonder at the confusion of corridors. They said, 'There is no way to come to the King!'"

"But the Prince threw open the door saying, 'Here he sits before you! All ways lead to the King!'"

Then Rabbi Israel added, "So we may find God."

In the afternoon, the Baal Shem Tov called the tavern-keeper.

"I will harness the horse at once!" said the tavern-keeper.

"No, not yet. First, we will eat the evening meal." Then the Rabbi and his students sat down again, and ate largely and well.

As evening came, the rabbi himself went to the barn and harnessed the horse to the wagon. "Now we will go," he said.

The inn-keeper got into the wagon with them.

"At last I will see what manner of horse he has here," he thought. And he bound his cloth around his throat, for he thought, "A great wind will come because of our swift riding."

The little horse began to walk. At first, the tavern-keeper saw, they were going along the same road on which his tavern stood. Every house along the way he knew, and every tree. But as the darkness grew like sleep around his eyes, he was no longer sure where he rode. First, there seemed to be no more houses. Then there seemed to be no more people. And at last, there seemed to be no more trees. He was awake, he listened, and yet he could not distinguish the hoofbeats of the horse. The wagon moved silently through the darkness, smoothly as if floating on a surface of glass. The air was tender about his face, and there was a sweet odour in his nostrils.

He thought to himself, "Perhaps I am not here at all!"

Then he felt the chassid who sat next to him, in order to make sure that this was no vision.

"Where are we going?" he said.

"We are going to Berlin."

"But I do not recognise the road!"

The Baal Shem Tov said, "This is a short way."

All night long they rode, and the tavern-keeper saw no light of habitation, saw nothing but the stars in the velvet sky, and heard nothing but the voices of the chassidim as they talked of things in the Torah.

The Rabbi himself spoke of many wonderful things. He spoke of the prophet Elijah, who wanders about the world, and of how at the time of Redemption he would bring down Messiah, and then at last the Shechina, the Glory of the Living God, will cease her wandering, and unite again with Him.

"No man can hasten the coming of that day," said the Master of the Word. "Even the mightiest of Words cannot bring down that day, as long as evil is among us."

Towards dawn, the inn-keeper began again to hear the hoofbeats of the horse. Then he felt the wagon jolting on a road. He saw trees, he saw houses. He saw that they were near a great city. And when they rode into the city, he saw that it was Berlin.

The tavern-keeper remembered that the Baal Shem Tov had said he was going to the house of a wealthy Jew to perform a wedding service. But now instead of driving to the street on which stood the houses of the rich, the Rabbi stopped before a humble guesthouse and went in there with his students, and they said their morning prayers, and sat themselves down at the table.

The tavern-keeper wandered out into the streets. He was restless, and filled with the news of the marvellous ride he had taken, and he wanted to find someone to tell of the great wonder.

He came to the street of rich houses. Each house was a veritable palace. And one of these houses, he saw, was festooned as for a great feast. As the tavern-keeper stood before this house, the door opened and a young man came running out of it. Though he ran in great haste, he did not seem to know where to go, but turned first one way and then the other way. His face was terribly wrought in grief.

The tavern-keeper saw that the young man was wearing Sabbath clothes and new shoes. "He is certainly the bridegroom," he thought.

The bridegroom ran up to the tavern-keeper and said, "Where is there a doctor?"

The tavern-keeper seized his arm and cried, "Come, I know of a rabbi who works wonders!"

But the bridegroom stood still, repeating to himself. "Of what use will it be? She is dead."

The tavern-keeper could not contain himself, and cried, "The rabbi can do all things! He came a hundred miles in one night, to perform a wedding in Berlin!"

The bridegroom said, "The bride is dead."

The tavern-keeper said, "His powers are so great, he can surely raise people from the dead! Come, I will take you to him!" The bridegroom put out his hand, and the inn-keeper led him to the Baal Shem Tov.

"Tell me what has happened," said the Master.

"Today, I was to have been married," said the man. "Last night there was a great festival in the house of the bride. All through the feast, she was joyous, she danced, she was the happiest of all the people in the house. We danced together at our wedding feast. Then she went up to her room and slept. And this morning when she awoke and tried to rise, she fell to the ground, dead."

"Take me to the house," said the Baal Shem Tov.

They came to the beautiful house that was festooned for the wedding. They went through the ballroom where the feast had been held, they went up the stairway and came into the maiden's bedroom. There, dressed in a long white robe, lay the body of the bride. Beside her on the bed lay the wedding-dress that she had begun to put upon herself.

The Baal Shem leaned over, and looked into the face of the girl. Then he said to the women who were in the room, "Dress her in her shroud." And he said to the men, "Dig a grave for her in the cemetery." And he said to the groom, "I will go with you to bury the bride. But you must do everything exactly as I order. Take her wedding-dress and her ornaments and her wedding-shoes, and bring them to the grave."

Then the women dressed the maiden for the grave. And when she was ready to be buried, they put her in a coffin. The bride-groom took her wedding-dress in his hands, and carried it with him as he walked beside the coffin.

Two grave-diggers had already made a hole in the earth. They straightened their backs, and prepared to climb out of the hole.

But the Baal Shem Tov called down to them, "Remain there, and do as I say. Let one of you stand at her head, and the other stand at her feet. Do not take your eyes from the face of the girl. And if a change comes over the face of the girl, I will give you a sign. Then lift her, and help her to rise."

They took the maiden as she lay in her shroud, and they put her down into the earth. They drew the cover away from her face, that the living might look the last time upon her. Her face was white as her shroud.

They did not throw earth over her body.

The Baal Shem Tov took his stick and leaned upon it, leaning over the open grave. His eyes looked into the face of the dead maiden. And all those who were there looked first at the face of the corpse, and then at the living face of the Baal Shem Tov. And as they watched his face, they saw that he had gone into another world. As they looked into his eyes, they could almost see what he saw in the other world. They knew that the Power was come over him, and that he was no longer among them. They saw his mouth move, and heard him speak words made of sounds they had never heard before. And none who were there by the grave could ever remember the Words that he had uttered.

Only the bridegroom kept his eyes upon the face of his beloved.

And after a long while, a shiver coursed through his back. For it seemed to him that he had seen a tinge of colour, delicate as the brush of an eyelid, pass upon her cheek.

In that same moment the Baal Shem Tov trembled with mighty force, as a man trembles who clutches with all his strength to hold back the wheels of a wagon that would break away and rush downhill. Then Rabbi Israel straightened himself, and breathed freely. He made a sign to the two men, and they lifted the girl out of the grave. Her eyes were open. She looked to her bridegroom, and smiled.

"Dress her in her wedding clothes, and take her under the canopy," said the Baal Shem Tov. "All that has happened, forget."

With these words, Rabbi Israel started to walk away. But the groom ran after him and begged him to be the one to say the wedding service.

For the wedding, the feast was prepared, greater than ever before. And the joy in that house was unbounded, for the bride had returned from the dead.

Only, all day long, when they asked of her, "What happened over there?" she became confused, and answered in a bewildered way, "I do not know. I do not know who he was!"

When the couple stood under the wedding canopy, and the Baal Shem Tov began to read the wedding service, the bride started joyfully and cried out, "It is he!"

Rabbi Israel whispered to her, "Be still!" and he finished the service.

But when the blessing was over the bride could no longer contain her secret. She would not let the Rabbi go away. "It was he who brought me back from over there!" she said. "I know him by his voice!"

Then, as they sat to eat the wedding meal, the bride told of all that had happened. The groom had been married once before. His first wife had been the aunt of this maiden, who was an orphan. The girl had lived happily in their house.

When the wife became sick, and knew that she was about to die, she called the girl to her bedside and said, "Promise me that you will never marry my husband. Otherwise, I cannot die in peace."

The maiden was afraid to make the promise, for she already felt stirring within her the love for her future groom. But because she could not deny the wish of the dying woman, she gave the promise that was asked of her.

Then the woman called her young husband to her bedside and said, "I cannot die peacefully unless you promise never to marry my niece." In order that she might die peacefully, he gave her his hand and his word.

But after the dead woman was taken from the house, the man and the girl were left there together. Each day, they knew their love to be stronger. At last they could no longer restrain their love, and they agreed to marry each other.

On the morning of the wedding day, as the maiden arose to put on her wedding garments, the angry soul of the dead woman came into the house. She seized the soul of the girl, crying, "You have broken your sacred promise! Come with me!"

And before the Almighty she demanded the death of the bride.

As the bride was placed in her grave, her soul went up for

judgement. The souls of the two women stood for judgement together. The soul of the first wife cried, "She has taken my beloved from me!"

And the soul of the maiden cried, "She has taken me from my beloved!"

At that moment, the Baal Shem Tov came up to the court of judgement. He placed himself between the two souls. "The dead have no right on earth!" he declared. "The right is with the living!"

He seized the soul of the girl, and drew it away from the soul of the dead woman. "The bride and groom are not guilty of wrong," he said. "The promise that they made was given against their wills. Their promise was made only to give peace to the soul of the dying woman. And now she must leave them in peace!"

The words of Rabbi Israel were judged to be right. And pronouncement was made, "Let the maiden's soul return to her body."

But the dead woman would not free the soul of the girl. She clung to the girl's soul with all her might.

"Let her go!" cried the Baal Shem Tov. And then he drew all his strength together and wrenched the soul of the maiden from the clutches of the dead woman's soul. "Let her go! Can't you see that the wedding canopy is waiting!"

That was when the bride returned to the living, and was taken out of her grave, and dressed in her wedding garments.

Adapted from Levin, M. (1932) *The Golden Mountain: Marvellous tales of Rabbi Israel Baal Shem Tov and of his Great-Grandson, Rabbi Nachmann*, retold from Hebrew, Yiddish and German sources. New York: Behrman House Inc. Publishers.

* * *

The Old Testament records only three instances where the newly dead return to life, all through contact with the prophets Elijah and Elisha. Elijah resuscitates the son of a widow in the Sidonian town of Zarepath, and Elisha does the same for the only son of his Shunamite hostess. The third concerns the restoration to life of a corpse on touching Elisha's bones. The first two stories share similarities with healing accounts from shamanistic societies. There is one important difference though, for the two prophets' powers are attributed to Yahweh, rather than to spirit helpers as would be the case if they were shamans (see Johnston, 2002, pp.220-221).

There is a wealth of scholarly literature on afterlife beliefs throughout the ancient Near East. The Egyptians, for example, had extensive views on the afterlife, which are recorded in the Pyramid Texts for the Old Kingdom (third millennia BCE), the Coffin Texts from the Middle Kingdom (early second millennium) and the Book of the Dead from the New Kingdom (mid-to-late second millennium), as well as in many other Books of the Netherworld from the New Kingdom and later' (see Johnston, 2002, pp.230-231).

From the Old Testament, however, we learn that Israelite life and faith were centred on the present life and relating to Yahweh in the here and now. Death was the end of this life, not the start of the next, and Sheol was regarded as a place of no return (Job 16:22), a place of captivity with gates (Is. 38:10) and bars (Jonah 2:6).

All this makes *The Bride in her Grave* something of a rarity. The suggestion that the bringing someone back from the dead might be achievable by a mere mortal would be regarded by Orthodox Jews as verging on the sacrilegious, though not to the followers of the Baal Shem Tov. For many of his disciples believed that he came from the Davidic line tracing its lineage to the royal house of King David, and by extension with the institution of the Jewish Messiah.

Reference:

Johnston, P.S. (2002) *Shades of Sheol: Death and Afterlife in the Old Testament*, Downers Grove, Illinois: interVarsity Press.

Hades in the eyes of the Ainu

The Ainu are an ethnic minority in Japan, living primarily on the northernmost Japanese island of Hokkaidō, although there were also small populations of Ainu living on the island of Sakhalin and in the Kuriles until the end of World War II, when the Soviet Union took control of Sakhalin and the Ainu there fled. Until the Meiji Restoration of 1868, when Japan took formal possession of Hokkaidō and began the systematic integration of the Ainu into the Japanese nation, the Ainu lived almost exclusively as hunter-gatherers north of the always advancing frontier of Japanese agriculture. As for Ainu literature, it was traditionally of an exclusively oral variety, and very little was reduced to writing in any language before the 19th century.

The Ainu believe that everything in nature has a *kamui* (spirit or god) on the inside, and there is a hierarchy of the *kamui*. The most important is grandmother earth (fire), then *kamui* of the mountain (animals), then *kamui* of the sea (sea animals), lastly everything else. The people give thanks to the gods before eating and, in times of sickness, pray to the deity of fire. They believe their spirits are immortal, and that their spirits will be rewarded when they leave this reality by ascending to *kamui mosir* (the Land of the Gods).

They have no priests by profession and the village chief performs whatever religious ceremonies are necessary; ceremonies are confined to making libations of rice beer, saying prayers, and offering willow sticks with wooden shavings attached to them. These sticks are called *inau* (singular) and *nusa* (plural). They are placed on an altar used to "send back" the spirits of killed animals.

The translator of the stories presented below, Basil Hall Chamberlain, was known as one of the pioneering interpreters of things Japanese in his time. (He also translated the Shinto classic

Kojiki). Like many philologists though, his interest in the Ainu was purely academic, centring mainly on the light that knowledge of the Ainu could shed on Japanese place-names and prehistory. Like many of the Japanese he lived and worked with, he had little regard for the Ainu, and his comments in the Prefatory Remarks to the collection these tales come from sound downright inflammatory today, representing a fine specimen of Victorian racism.

The Hunter in Hades

A handsome and brave young man, who was skilful in the chase, one day pursued a large bear into the recesses of the mountains. On and on ran the bear, and still the young fellow pursued it up heights and crags more and more dangerous, but without ever being able to get near enough to shoot it with his poisoned arrows. At last, on a bleak mountain-summit, the bear disappeared down a hole in the ground. The young man followed it in, and found himself in an immense cavern, at the far end of which was a gleam of light. Towards this he groped his way, and, on emerging, found himself in another world. Everything there was as in the world of men, but more beautiful. There were trees, houses, villages, human beings. With these, however, the young hunter had no concern. What he wanted was his bear, which had totally disappeared. The best plan seemed to be to seek it in the remoter mountain district of this new world underground. So he followed up a valley; and, being tired and hungry, picked the grapes and mulberries that were hanging to the trees, and ate them as he trudged along.

Happening suddenly, for some reason or other, to look down upon his own body, what was not his horror to find himself transformed into a serpent! His very cries and groans, on making the discovery, were turned into serpent's hisses. What was he to do? To go back like this to his native world, where snakes are hated, would be certain death. No plan presented itself to his mind. But, unconsciously, he wandered, or rather crept and glided, back to the entrance of the cavern that led home to the world of men; and there, at the foot of a pine-tree of extraordinary size and height, he fell asleep.

To him then, in a dream, appeared the goddess of the pine-tree, and said: "I am sorry to see you in this state. Why did you eat of the poisonous fruits of Hades? The only thing you can do to recover your proper shape is to climb to the top of this pine-tree, and fling yourself down. Then you may, perhaps, become a human being again."

On waking from this dream, the young man,—or rather snake, as he still found himself to be,—was filled half with hope and half with fear. But he resolved to follow the goddess' advice. So, gliding up the tall pine-tree, he reached its topmost branch, and, after hesitating a few moments, flung himself down. Crash he went. On coming to his senses, he found himself standing at the foot of the tree; and close by was the body of an immense serpent, ripped open so as to allow of his having crawled out of it. After offering up thanks to the pine-tree, and setting up the divine symbols in its honour, he hastened to retrace his steps through the long, tunnel-like cavern, through which he had originally entered Hades. After walking for a certain time, he emerged into the world of men, to find himself on the mountain-top, whither he had pursued the bear which he had never seen again.

On reaching his home, he went to bed, and dreamt a second time. It was the same goddess of the pine-tree that appeared before him and said: "I have come to tell you that you cannot stay long in the world of men after once eating the grapes and mulberries of Hades. There is a goddess in Hades who wishes to marry you. She it was who, assuming the form of a bear, lured you into the cavern, and thence to the under-world. You must make up your mind to come away."

And so it fell out. The young man awoke; but a grave sickness overpowered him. A few days later he went a second time to Hades, and returned no more to the land of the living. (Written down from memory).

Told by Ishanashte, 22nd July, 1886, and taken from Chamberlain, B. H. (1888) *Aino Folk-tales*. With an Introduction by Edward B. Tylor, London.

An Inquisitive Man's Experience of Hades

Three generations before my time there lived an Aino who wished to find out whether the stories told about the existence of an underworld were true. So one day he penetrated into an immense cavern (since washed away by the waves) at the river-mouth of Sarubutsu. All was dark in front, all was dark behind. But at last there was a glimmer of light a-head. The man went on, and soon emerged into Hades. There were trees, and villages, and rivers, and the sea, and large junks loading fish and seaweed. Some of the people were Ainos, some were Japanese, just as in the every-day world. Among the number were some whom he had known when they were alive. But, though *he* saw *them, they,*— strange to say,—did not seem to see *him.* Indeed he was invisible to all, excepting to the dogs; for dogs see everything, even spirits, and the dogs of Hades barked at him fiercely. Hereupon the people of the place, judging that some evil spirit had come among them, threw him dirty food, such as evil spirits eat, in order, as they thought, to appease him. Of course he was disgusted, and flung the filthy fish-bones and soiled rice away. But every time that he did so the stuff immediately returned to the pocket in his bosom, so that he was greatly distressed.

At last, entering a fine-looking house near the beach, he found his father and mother, not old—as they were when they died— but in the heyday of youth and strength. He called to his mother, but she ran away trembling. He clasped his father by the hand, and said: "Father! Don't you know me? Can't you see me? I am your son." But his father fell yelling to the ground. So he stood aloof again, and watched how his parents and the other people in the house set up the divine symbols, and prayed in order to make the evil spirit depart.

In his despair at being unrecognised he did depart, with the unclean offerings that had been made to him still sticking to his person, notwithstanding his endeavours to get rid of them. It was only when, after passing back through the cavern, he had emerged once more into the world of men, that they left him free from their pollution. He returned home, and never wished to visit Hades again. It is a foul place (Written down from memory).

Told by Ishanashte, 22nd July, 1886, and taken from Chamberlain, B. H. (1888) *Aino Folk-tales*, London.

The Bridge of Sighs

The Bridge of Sighs (Italian: *Ponte dei Sospiri*) is a bridge in Venice. The enclosed bridge is made of white limestone and has windows with stone bars. It passes over the Rio di Palazzo and connects the old prisons to the interrogation rooms in the Doge's Palace. It was designed by Antoni Contino (whose uncle Antonio da Ponte designed the Rialto Bridge), and built in 1602.

The view from the Bridge of Sighs was the last view of Venice that convicts saw before their imprisonment. The bridge name, given by Lord Byron in the 19th century, comes from the suggestion that prisoners would sigh at their final view of beautiful Venice out the window before being taken down to their cells. In reality, the days of inquisitions and summary executions were over by the time the bridge was built and the cells under the palace roof were occupied mostly by small-time criminals. In addition, little could be seen from inside the Bridge due to the stone grills covering the windows. A local legend says that lovers will be granted everlasting love and bliss if they kiss on a gondola at sunset under the bridge and be in love and happily married to a blissful husband or wife for the rest of your life.

There is also a "Bridge of Sighs" that can be found in Oxford, and yet another in Cambridge. The Hertford Bridge in Oxford is often referred to as the Bridge of Sighs because of its supposed similarity to the famous one in Venice. However, it was never actually intended to be a replica of the Venetian bridge, and indeed it bears a closer resemblance to the Rialto Bridge in the same city. There is a false legend saying that many decades ago, a survey of the health of students was taken, and as Hertford College's students were the heaviest, the college closed off the bridge to force them to take the stairs, giving them extra exercise. However, if the bridge is not used, the students actually climb fewer stairs than if they do use the bridge.

The Cambridge "Bridge of Sighs" came into being because the building of New Court made necessary a second crossing of the river between it and Third Court, and New Court's architect seized the opportunity for some more charming and allusive romanticism. It must be noted, however, that the only real similarity between the Bridge of Sighs and its Venetian namesake is that both of them are covered bridges. Today it is part of the main thoroughfare through St John's College in Cambridge and used daily by those who live and work here.

The bridge in Venice inspired a certain Thomas Hood (1798–1845) to write a poem, which is presented below and was taken from Quiller-Couch, A. (ed.) (1919) *The Oxford Book of English Verse: 1250–1900*. As you will see for yourself, it can hardly be regarded as a masterpiece, and is much more likely to bring to mind the poetry of William Topaz McGonagall of Dundee (1825-1902), who has been widely hailed as the writer of the worst poetry in the English language:

The Bridge of Sighs

ONE more Unfortunate,
  Weary of breath,
Rashly importunate,
  Gone to her death!

Take her up tenderly,   5
  Lift her with care;
Fashion'd so slenderly
  Young, and so fair!

Look at her garments
Clinging like cerements;   10
Whilst the wave constantly

Drips from her clothing;
Take her up instantly,
  Loving, not loathing.

Touch her not scornfully;   15
Think of her mournfully,
  Gently and humanly;
Not of the stains of her,
All that remains of her
  Now is pure womanly.   20

Make no deep scrutiny
Into her mutiny
  Rash and undutiful:
Past all dishonour,
Death has left on her   25
  Only the beautiful.

Still, for all slips of hers,
  One of Eve's family —
Wipe those poor lips of hers
  Oozing so clammily.   30

Loop up her tresses
  Escaped from the comb,
Her fair auburn tresses;
Whilst wonderment guesses
  Where was her home?   35

Who was her father?
  Who was her mother?
Had she a sister?
  Had she a brother?
Or was there a dearer one   40

Still, and a nearer one
  Yet, than all other?

Alas! for the rarity
Of Christian charity
  Under the sun!   45
O, it was pitiful!
Near a whole city full,
  Home she had none.

Sisterly, brotherly,
Fatherly, motherly   50
  Feelings had changed:
Love, by harsh evidence,
Thrown from its eminence;
Even God's providence
  Seeming estranged.   55

Where the lamps quiver
So far in the river,
  With many a light
From window and casement,
From garret to basement,   60
She stood, with amazement,
  Houseless by night.

The bleak wind of March
  Made her tremble and shiver;
But not the dark arch,   65
Or the black flowing river:
Mad from life's history,
Glad to death's mystery,
  Swift to be hurl'd—
Anywhere, anywhere   70

Out of the world!

In she plunged boldly—
No matter how coldly
  The rough river ran—
Over the brink of it,   75
Picture it—think of it,
  Dissolute Man!
Lave in it, drink of it,
  Then, if you can!

Take her up tenderly,   80
  Lift her with care;
Fashion'd so slenderly,
  Young, and so fair!

Ere her limbs frigidly
Stiffen too rigidly,   85
  Decently, kindly,
Smooth and compose them;
And her eyes, close them,
  Staring so blindly!

Dreadfully staring   90
  Thro' muddy impurity,
As when with the daring
Last look of despairing
  Fix'd on futurity.

Perishing gloomily,   95
Spurr'd by contumely,
Cold inhumanity,
Burning insanity,
  Into her rest.—

Cross her hands humbly   *100*
As if praying dumbly,
  Over her breast!

Owning her weakness,
  Her evil behaviour,
And leaving, with meekness,   *105*
  Her sins to her Saviour!

In fact, McGonagall himself wrote a poem about a bridge, probably the poem he is best remembered for. And this, as you are now about to see for yourself, is because it succeeds in turning a genuine tragedy into what unfortunately amounts to what can only be described as a comedy as a result of its ridiculous rhymes:

The Tay Bridge Disaster

Beautiful Railway Bridge of the Silv'ry Tay!
Alas! I am very sorry to say
That ninety lives have been taken away
On the last Sabbath day of 1879,
Which will be remember'd for a very long time.
'Twas about seven o'clock at night,
And the wind it blew with all its might,
And the rain came pouring down,
And the dark clouds seem'd to frown,
And the Demon of the air seem'd to say—
"I'll blow down the Bridge of Tay."
When the train left Edinburgh
The passengers' hearts were light and felt no sorrow,
But Boreas blew a terrific gale,
Which made their hearts for to quail,
And many of the passengers with fear did say—

"I hope God will send us safe across the Bridge of Tay."
But when the train came near to Wormit Bay,
Boreas he did loud and angry bray,
And shook the central girders of the Bridge of Tay
On the last Sabbath day of 1879,
Which will be remember'd for a very long time.
So the train sped on with all its might,
And Bonnie Dundee soon hove in sight,
And the passengers' hearts felt light,
Thinking they would enjoy themselves on the New Year,
With their friends at home they lov'd most dear,
And wish them all a happy New Year.
So the train mov'd slowly along the Bridge of Tay,
Until it was about midway,
Then the central girders with a crash gave way,
And down went the train and passengers into the Tay!
The Storm Fiend did loudly bray,
Because ninety lives had been taken away,
On the last Sabbath day of 1879,
Which will be remember'd for a very long time.
As soon as the catastrophe came to be known
The alarm from mouth to mouth was blown,
And the cry rang out all o'er the town,
Good Heavens! the Tay Bridge is blown down,
And a passenger train from Edinburgh,
Which fill'd all the peoples hearts with sorrow,
And made them for to turn pale,
Because none of the passengers were sav'd to tell the tale
How the disaster happen'd on the last Sabbath day of 1879,
Which will be remember'd for a very long time.
It must have been an awful sight,
To witness in the dusky moonlight,
While the Storm Fiend did laugh, and angry did bray,
Along the Railway Bridge of the Silv'ry Tay,

Oh! ill-fated Bridge of the Silv'ry Tay,
I must now conclude my lay
By telling the world fearlessly without the least dismay,
That your central girders would not have given way,
At least many sensible men do say,
Had they been supported on each side with buttresses,
At least many sensible men confesses,
For the stronger we our houses do build,
The less chance we have of being killed.

The Dead Bride

There lived a man in the land of Ku'ñe, right opposite the island Ima'lik (one of the Diomede Islands). One day he was going to perform the thanksgiving ceremonial, because he was a good sea-hunter, had killed many whales, and fed all his neighbours. So he prepared everything in his house.

He placed the tips of whale-flippers upon a skin. Then all at once a thong-seal jumped out of the water-hole upon the ice. The village stood high up on the cape, and people were walking along the shore on either side of it. That man had on neither cap nor belt, because he was changing his clothes for the ceremonial. He rushed down to the water-hole just as he stood.

When he was quite close, the thong-seal plunged into the hole, and in a few moments jumped out of another hole. This was one of its breathing-holes. The man pursued it. The thong-seal turned to still another hole, and plunged down. The man stood close by the hole, watching for it to come up. When he looked down into the water, he saw a woman's face—the face of a daughter of an American Eskimo. Her father was a rich trader. She had died, and had been carried away to the funeral-place. After the funeral, she had left her grave to get a husband.

While the man of Ku'ñe was standing there, the woman approached the surface. Her long tresses were floating on the water. She shook off the water, then she caught the man and carried him away to her own land. When they came to the shore, he saw a large house; but, on looking with closer attention, he ascertained that it was only a wooden lodge for the dead, like those the people of the other shore construct. In the lodge lay a corpse. He felt much afraid. Unexpectedly the corpse sat up and drew a deep sigh. "Oh, oh, oh! I slept too long, I feel quite benumbed." It was the corpse of a woman. She stretched her arms and legs and shoulders, making the joints click in order to regain their suppleness. "Now let us go to my father!" said she.

They did so. Her father was arranging a religious ceremonial. They stood in the rear of the house. The house was full of shamans. They performed various acts of magic. Some were calling the Upper Gods; others, to'maraks and the deceased; still others were calling the sea-gods. Thus they were calling, — one this being, one that.

A young shaman, though having no "living voices," [ventriloquistic ability] still a very great shaman, was sitting there silent. The old man asked him to practise also. "I am grieving deeply for my dead daughter. You must sing and cheer me up." — "I cannot sing, I have no voices, I know no songs." — "That is all right. Sing some other man's songs." — "Well, then, I will try." He began to sing, "I am practising shamanistic art within the house, while the others are practising too. I am practising within the house."

"There," he said, "I see her standing in the rear of the house. But this one, the man of Ku'ñe—why does he stand close to her?" Thus, being a great shaman, he saw them. Oh, the father felt much joy! He said, "I will give you triple payment. One shall be the boat; another, the harpoon-line; the third, the harpoon—three payments of great value." — "All right!" Then the dead bride said to her future husband, "Let us climb to the roof of the house! Otherwise he will catch us." They climbed to the roof; and the young shaman sang again, "I practise within the house, while the others are practising too. I practise within the house. Whoop!" He drew a deep breath, and with it he drew them into the house. He stretched the skirt of his coat and caught them in it. "Here they are!" The father was much pleased. He kissed his daughter and greeted his son-in-law. They passed a winter there. The next summer they returned in a boat to the land of Ku'ñe.

Told by Ñipe'wġi, an Asiatic Eskimo man, in the village of Uñi'sak, at Indian Point, May, 1901, and taken from Bogoras, W.

(1913) *The Eskimo of Siberia*, Leiden & New York. In *The Jessup North Pacific Expedition* Edited by Franz Boas Volume VIII.

Waldemar Bogoras was an exiled Russian revolutionary, who became an ethnographer during his involuntary "field experience" in Siberia where was sent for his anti-governmental activities. It is possible that the marginal status of political exiles like Bogoras actually worked to their advantage in that it might have helped to create a spiritual bond between them and the Siberian natives, who were themselves marginalised and put down (see Znamenski, 2007, p.74). Bogoras was a Polish-Jew who served his term of exile in the far north-eastern tundra. Before the revolution, he had managed to get round the laws that made it hard for Jews to live in Petersburg by declaring himself to be a convert to Lutheranism. Then, ironically, in 1936, "having done his best to turn himself into an orthodox Marxist, 71-year-old Bogoras was taken into custody by the NKVD and never seen again" (Reid, 2003, p.165).

At the time when Bogoras did his fieldwork, shamanism was associated with little more than backwardness and insanity, a situation that only really changed when Eliade's seminal work, *Shamanism and Archaic Techniques of Ecstasy* was first published in 1951. This had the effect of rehabilitating shamanism, and stretched out the geographic borders of shamanism so that it came to be applied to "all non-Western and pre-Christian European spiritualities which did not fit the format of organised world religions and in which spiritual practitioners worked in altered states" (Znamenski, 2009, p.197).

The American anthropologist Michael Harner, and a student whose doctoral thesis he examined, Carlos Castaneda, were greatly influenced by Eliade, and in the 1960s this resulted in the development of what is known as neo-shamanism - a Western spirituality that capitalised on the Eliadean vision. If we are to include this practice under the heading of shamanism, traditional definitions of shamanism can no longer be applied, and a new model is called for.

Existing models of shamanism have tended to focus upon particular skills or states of consciousness exhibited by shamans and are therefore framed with reference to outcomes, rather than by attending to the processes of development leading to them. David Gordon Wilson, New College, Edinburgh in his paper "Spiritualist Mediums and other Traditional Shamans: Towards an Apprenticeship Model of Shamanic Practice," (BASR Conference 2010) proposes an apprenticeship model as the basis of a new definition of shamanism. This, he argues, offers a distinctive, clearly-structured approach to understanding the acquisition and nature of shamanic skills, without being unduly prescriptive as to which particular shamanic skills should be anticipated in any given cultural setting. Not all shamans, however, necessarily accept apprentices—the *nayogh* [which translates as "people who are looking"] in Armenia today certainly do not, to give but one example. This is because it is believed that a person can only become a *nayogh* if they receive a calling, and not by becoming an apprentice to one. They will, however, sometimes pass on prayers that they use, though only through a member of the opposite sex. So if a married woman wanted a prayer, for example, it would be given to her husband by the *nayogh* to be passed on to her. Therefore, unless the apprenticeship can be regarded as taking place through what might consist of nothing more than a single vision, using such a model to describe the acquisition of all shamanic skills would not seem to be particularly helpful.

Another problem that arises when attempting to arrive at a satisfactory definition which can encompass all the different forms of shamanism is that in some cultures each practitioner develops his or her own approach to healing, which may include going into a genuine trance state, going into an imitative trance state, a demonstration of tricks, or a mixture of all three practices. And once again, this applies to the Armenian *nayogh*. So any definition of what being a shaman entails clearly needs to take such differences into account too. The following definition is therefore proposed:

A shaman is someone who performs an ecstatic (in a trance state), imitative, or demonstrative ritual of a séance (or a combination of all three), at will (in other words, whenever he or she chooses to do so), in which aid is sought from beings in (what are considered to be) other realities generally for healing purposes or for divination—both for individuals and / or the community.

As for the practice of shamanism, it is understood to encompass a personalistic view of the world, in which life is seen to be not only about beliefs and practices, but also about relationships—how we are related, and how we relate to each other. In shamanism the notion of interdependence "is the idea of the kinship of all life, the recognition that nothing can exist in and of itself without being in relationship to other things, and therefore that it is insane for us to consider ourselves as essentially unrelated parts of the whole Earth" (Halifax in Nicholson, 1987, p.220). And we now have proof of our interdependence:

[I]t has been shown that during mystical ecstasy (or its equivalent, entheogenic shamanic states [states induced by ingesting hallucinogens]), the individual experiences a blurring of the boundaries on the ego and feels at "one with Nature"; the ego is no longer confined within the body, but extends outward to all of Nature; other living beings come to share in the ego, as an authentic communion with the environment, which is sensed as in some way divine (Ruck, Staples, et al., 2007, p.76).

Further justification for the belief that all life is connected can be found in the fact that the elementary particles that make up all matter, by their gravitational, electromagnetic or nuclear field, are coextensive with the whole universe, and as man is composed of these particles, he must therefore be in union with the entire cosmos.

The phrase "a religion of ritual observance" has been used in particular to describe Shinto—"a religion not of theology but of ritual observance" (Driver, 1991, p.38).

However, other religions, apart from Shinto, could also be listed under this heading, Wicca for example. As in the case of Shinto, there is no one bible or prayer book in Wicca and the primary concern is not ethics, dogma, or theology. Rather, it is a religion of ritual practice. These practices include marking eight holiday "sabbats" in the "wheel of the year", falling on the solstices, equinoxes and the four "cross quarter days" on or about the first of February, May, August and November. Many Wiccans also mark "esbats," rituals for worship in accordance with a given moon phase (such as the night of the full moon). The same clearly applies to shamanism too.

Additionally, shamanism can be seen to be a kinship-based religion, in which kinship is not only understood to involve extended family links between members, but also, in the case of neo-shamanism, links between people who regard themselves as members of a particular community—neo-shamanic practitioners who regularly participate in a drumming group, for example. To complicate matters even further, though, there are also those who choose to work entirely on their own.

So what we are in effect dealing with is a kinship-based religion of ritual observance that in different cultures takes on different forms, and one that can even take on a variety of different forms within the same culture, as is the case in present-day Armenia. And the definition being proposed here, unlike one based on an apprenticeship model or one that requires the shaman to perform an ecstatic ritual of a séance, has the advantage of being a comprehensive one; for it not only embraces all the forms of shamanism that have been practised, but also all the forms of shamanism that are being practised today.

References

Berman, M. (2007) *The Nature of Shamanism and the Shamanic Story*, Newcastle: Cambridge Scholars Publishing. (For the definition of Shamanism)

Berman, M, (2010) *Guided Visualisations through the Caucasus*, Pendraig Publishing. (For the information on neo-paganism in Armenia)

Driver, T.F. (1991) *The Magic of Ritual*, New York: Harper Collins Publishers.

Halifax, J. (1987) "Shamanism, Mind, and No Self" in Nicholson, S. (comp.) *Shamanism: An Expanded View of Reality*, Wheaton: The Theosophical Publishing House.

Reid, Anna (2003) *The Shaman's Coat: A Native History of Siberia*, London: Phoenix (first published in 2002 by Weidenfield and Nicolson).

Ruck, Carl A.P., Staples, B.D., Celdran J.A.G., Hoffman, M.A. (2007) *The Hidden World: Survival of Pagan Shamanic Themes in European Fairytales*, North Carolina: Carolina Academic Press.

Znamenski, A.A. (2007) *The Beauty of the Primitive: Shamanism and the Western*

Imagination, Oxford: Oxford University Press.

Znamenski, Andrei. (2009) 'Quest for Primal Knowledge: Mircea Eliade, Traditionalism, and "Archaic Techniques of Ecstasy"' In SHAMAN Vol. 17 Numbers 1 and 2, Budapest: Molnar & Kelemen Oriental Publishers.

The Resuscitation of the Only Daughter

There once lived an old couple who had an only daughter. She was a beautiful girl, and was very much courted by the young men of the tribe, but she said that she preferred single life, and to all their heart-touching tales of deep affection for her she always had one answer. That was "No."

One day this maiden fell ill and day after day grew worse. All the best medicine men were called in, but their medicines were of no avail, and in two weeks from the day that she was taken ill she lay a corpse. Of course there was great mourning in the camp. They took her body several miles from camp and rolled it in fine robes and blankets, then they laid her on a scaffold which they had erected. (This was the custom of burial among the Indians). They placed four forked posts into the ground and then lashed strong poles lengthwise and across the ends and made a bed of willows and stout ash brush. This scaffold was from five to seven feet from the ground. After the funeral the parents gave away all of their horses, fine robes and blankets and all of the belongings of the dead girl. Then they cut their hair off close to their heads, and attired themselves in the poorest apparel they could secure.

When a year had passed the friends and relatives of the old couple tried in vain to have them set aside their mourning. "You have mourned long enough," they would say. "Put aside your mourning and try and enjoy a few more pleasures of this life while you live. You are both growing old and can't live very many more years, so make the best of your time." The old couple would listen to their advice and then shake their heads and answer: "We have nothing to live for. Nothing we could join in would be any amusement to us, since we have lost the light of our lives."

So the old couple continued their mourning for their lost idol.

Two years had passed since the death of the beautiful girl, when one evening a hunter and his wife passed by the scaffold which held the dead girl. They were on their return trip and were heavily loaded down with game, and therefore could not travel very fast. About half a mile from the scaffold a clear spring burst forth from the side of a bank, and from this trickled a small stream of water, moistening the roots of the vegetation bordering its banks, and causing a growth of sweet green grass. At this spring the hunter camped and tethering his horses, at once set about helping his wife to erect the small tepee which they carried for convenience in travelling.

When it became quite dark, the hunter's dogs set up a great barking and growling. "Look out and see what the dogs are barking at," said the hunter to his wife. She looked out through the door and then drew back saying: "There is the figure of a woman advancing from the direction of the girl's scaffold." "I expect it is the dead girl; let her come, and don't act as if you were afraid," said the hunter. Soon they heard footsteps advancing and the steps ceased at the door. Looking down at the lower part of the door the hunter noticed a pair of small moccasins, and knowing that it was the visitor, said: "Whoever you are, come in and have something to eat."

At this invitation the figure came slowly in and sat down by the door with head covered and with a fine robe drawn tightly over the face. The woman dished up a fine supper and placing it before the visitor, said: "Eat, my friend, you must be hungry." The figure never moved, nor would it uncover to eat. "Let us turn our back towards the door and our visitor may eat the food," said the hunter. So his wife turned her back towards the visitor and made herself very busy cleaning the small pieces of meat that were hanging to the back sinews of the deer which had been killed. (This the Indians use as thread.) The hunter, filling his pipe, turned away and smoked in silence. Finally the dish was pushed back to the woman, who took it and after washing it, put it away. The figure still sat at the door, not a sound coming from it, neither was it breathing. The hunter at last said: "Are you the girl that was placed upon that scaffold two years ago?" It bowed its head two or three times in assent. "Are you going to sleep here tonight; if you are, my wife will make down a bed for you." The figure shook its head. "Are you going to come again tomorrow night to us?" It nodded assent.

For three nights in succession the figure visited the hunter's camp. The third night the hunter noticed that the figure was breathing. He saw one of the hands protruding from the robe. The skin was perfectly black and was stuck fast to the bones of the hand. On seeing this the hunter arose and going over to his medicine sack which hung on a pole, took down the sack and, opening it, took out some roots and mixing them with skunk oil and vermillion, said to the figure:

"If you will let us rub your face and hands with this medicine it will put new life into the skin and you will assume your complexion again and it will put flesh on you." The figure assented and the hunter rubbed the medicine on her hands and face. Then she arose and walked back to the scaffold. The next day the hunter moved camp towards the home village. That night he camped within a few miles of the village. When night came,the dogs, as usual, set up a great barking, and looking out, the wife saw the girl approaching.

When the girl had entered and sat down, the hunter noticed that the girl did not keep her robe so closely together over her face. When the wife gave her something to eat, the girl reached out and took the dish, thus exposing her hands, which they at once noticed were again natural. After she had finished her meal, the hunter said: "Did my medicine help you?" She nodded assent. "Do you want my medicine rubbed all over your body?"

Again she nodded. "I will mix enough to rub your entire body, and I will go outside and let my wife rub it on for you." He mixed a good supply and going out left his wife to rub the girl.

When his wife had completed the task she called to her husband to come in, and when he came in he sat down and said to the girl: "Tomorrow we will reach the village. Do you want to go with us?" She shook her head. "Will you come again to our camp tomorrow night after we have camped in the village?" She nodded her head in assent. "Then do you want to see your parents?" She nodded again, and arose and disappeared into the darkness.

Early the next morning the hunter broke camp and travelled far into the afternoon, when he arrived at the village. He instructed his wife to go at once and inform the old couple of what had happened. The wife did so and at sunset the old couple came to the hunter's tepee. They were invited to enter and a fine supper was served them. Soon after they had finished their supper the dogs of the camp set up a great barking. "Now she is coming, so be brave and you will soon see your lost daughter," said the hunter. Hardly had he finished speaking when she entered the tent as natural as ever she was in life. Her parents clung to her and smothered her with kisses.

They wanted her to return home with them, but she would stay with the hunter who had brought her back to life, and she married him, becoming his second wife. A short time after taking the girl for his wife, the hunter joined a war party and never returned, as he was killed on the battlefield.

A year after her husband's death she married again. This husband was also killed by a band of enemies whom the warriors were pursuing for stealing some of their horses. The third husband also met a similar fate to the first. He was killed on the field of battle.

She was still a handsome woman at the time of the third husband's death, but never again married, as the men feared her, saying she was holy, and that any one who married her would be sure to be killed by the enemy.

So she took to doctoring the sick and gained the reputation of being the most skilled doctor in the nation. She lived to a ripe old age and when she felt death approaching she had them take her to where she had rested once before, and crawling to the top of the newly erected scaffold, wrapped her blankets and robes about her, covered her face carefully, and fell into that sleep from which there is no more awakening.

Taken from McLaughlin, M. L. (1913) *Myths and Legends of the Sioux*, http://www.gutenberg.org/files/341/341.txt [accessed 27/08/2010]

The collector of the book of tales this story comes from, Marie L. McLaughlin, was partly Sioux herself. Her maternal grandfather, Captain Duncan Graham, who had seen service in the British Army, was one of a party of Scotch Highlanders who in 1811 arrived in the British Northwest by way of York Factory, Hudson Bay, to found what was known as Selkirk Colony, near Lake Winnipeg, now within the province of Manitoba, Canada. Soon after his arrival at Lake Winnipeg he proceeded up the western fork of the Red River of the North to its source, and then down the Minnesota River to Mendota, the confluence of the Minnesota and Mississippi Rivers, where he met her grandmother, Ha-za-ho-ta-win, who was a full-blood of the Medawakanton Band of the Sioux Tribe.

Marie herself was born December 8, 1842, at Wabasha, Minnesota, and the man who became her husband, Major James McLaughlin, was Indian agent at Devils Lake Agency. In 1881 he was transferred to Standing Rock, on the Missouri River, then a very important agency, to take charge of the Sioux who had then but recently surrendered to the military authorities, and been brought by steamboat from various points on the upper Missouri, to be permanently located on the Standing Rock reservation.

Having been born and brought up in an Indian community, at

an early age Marie acquired a thorough knowledge of the Sioux language, and living on Indian reservations for most of her life, she was ideally placed to learn the legends and folk-lore of the people. The stories she collected were told to her by the older men and women of the Sioux, of which she made careful notes, conscious of the fact that if not recorded, they would probably have been lost forever.

Story of Thomas the Rhymer

For crossing over, there is a price to pay, for time on the other side is not what it seems to be as the two fiddlers in the following tale find out. It is based on Child Ballad 37, which is traceable back at least as far as the 13th century and there are several different variants of the story. Most, however, have the same basic theme—that Thomas either kissed or had sex with the Queen of Fairyland and either rode with her or was otherwise transported to Fairyland. One version relates that she changed into a hag immediately after sleeping with him, as some sort of a punishment to him, but returned to her originally beautiful state when they neared her castle, where her husband lived. Thomas stayed at a party in the castle, until she told him to return with her, coming into the mortal realm only to realise seven years had passed (a significant number in magic). He asked for a token to remember the Queen by, and was then offered the choice of being a harper or a prophet, and chose the latter. He became known as true Thomas, because he could not tell a lie, and was popularly supposed to have prophesised many great events in Scottish history. His gift of prophecy seems to have been related to that of poetry, as Thomas was a noted poet (hence, "Rhymer"), and was supposed to have written the ballad of *St Tristram*. After a number of years had passed Thomas returned to fairyland, where he is still said to be.

Human intercourse with the Fairies often led to the victim vanishing from the sight of his fellow beings for, it may be, centuries, during which period he was entertained in Fairyland, and to him it appeared as though only one night had passed. Thomas the Rhymer was an instance of this in Scotland, and there is a tale regarding the Welsh Fairies as follows:

Early one fine summer morning a young man had no sooner left an adjacent farmhouse than he heard a little bird singing most sweetly on a tree near at hand. Enchanted by the song he sat down to listen to it. When it ceased he arose, supposing, as would be thought natural, that only a few minutes had elapsed, but what was his astonishment to see the tree under which he had sat all withered and dead. On returning to the house he saw it changed also, with only an old man, a stranger to him, within it. On asking the old man what he was doing there, the latter angrily asked who it was who dared to insult him in his own house. "In your own house! Where's my father and mother," said the young man, "whom I left here a few minutes since, while I listened to the most charming music under yon tree, which, when I arose, was withered and leafless, and all things, too, seemed changed?" "Under the tree! Music! What's your name?" "John" said he. "Poor John," exclaimed the old man, "I heard my grandfather, who was your father, often speak of you, and long did he bewail your absence; fruitless enquiries were made of you, but old Catti Madlen, of Brechfa, said that you were under the power of Fairies, and would not be released until the last sap of that Sycamore was dried up. Embrace, embrace, my dear uncle, your nephew." The old man then attempted to embrace him, but at that moment he crumbled into dust (Porteous, 2002, p.104).

Records show that the character of Thomas in the ballad was in fact based on a historical figure. Thomas Learmonth (c. 1220 – c.1298; also spelled Learmount, Learmont, or Learmounth), better known as Thomas the Rhymer or True Thomas, was a 13th century Scottish laird and reputed prophet from Earlston (then called "Erceldoune"). On the southern edge of the village there are the remains of an old keep dating back to the 1400s, called "Rhymer's Tower" because they are believed to stand on the site of the castle originally built by Thomas the Rhymer.

Thomas the Rhymer's reputation for making prophesies is said to include a prediction of the death of Alexander III in a fall from a horse in 1286. This prediction was apparently made to the Earl of March in Dunbar Castle the day before the accident happened. According to some sources Thomas is also said to have had other supernatural powers that even rivalled those of Merlin. It is said that on visiting Fyvie Castle in Aberdeenshire, a freak gust of wind shut the gates in his face, and in response he placed the "curse of the weeping stones" on the castle, a curse which has led to problems of succession down through the centuries as an unusually large number of different families have occupied the castle.

On another occasion he is reputed to have prophesied that the "The Burn o' Breid sall rin fu' reid", which translates as "The river of bread shall run fully red". On 23rd June 1314 the English were heavily defeated by the Scots at the Battle of Bannockburn (Bannock=Scottish flatbread, burn=river). It was reported that for three weeks afterwards it was possible to cross the Bannockburn on English bodies without getting ones feet wet. Prophecy fulfilled.

The spot where Thomas is believed to have fallen asleep under the Eildon Tree is now marked by the Rhymer's Stone. It was erected by the Melrose Literary Society, and on it you will find the following inscription: "This stone marks the site of the Eildon Tree where legend says Thomas the Rhymer met the Queen of the Fairies and where he was inspired to utter the first notes of the Scottish muse.

This inscription, on what is believed to be Thomas Rhymer's family tombstone, can be found on the east wall of Earlston Kirk, and reads "Auld Rymer's Race, lyes in this place". Although the current church was built in 1892 by Rodgers, a firm still in existence in the village today, it's likely that the stone was removed from previous churches that had been on the site and then rebuilt into new ones. The current church is the fourth or possibly fifth on the site.

In the context of the spiritual interpretation of entry into fairyland, whichever method the fairy employed to bring the human into their world, and for whatever reason they wanted them there, the fairy would have been, in effect, desiring and appropriating (for a given length of time) the human spirit or soul. In the same context, those individuals who were tempted to enter fairyland voluntarily, for whatever reason, would have been aware that their visit amounted to a temporary, albeit tacit, commitment of their soul to (be used/enjoyed by) the fairies—a transaction which amounted to an implicit contract (Wilby, 2005, p.104).

In the case of Thomas Rhymer, for example, he was tempted into fairyland by his love for a fairy woman, and the two fiddlers by their love of money.

* * *

At the beginning of each summer, when the milk-white hawthorn is in bloom, anointing the air with its sweet odour, and miles and miles of golden whin adorn the glens and hill-slopes, the fairies come forth in grand procession, headed by the Fairy Queen. They are mounted on little white horses, and when on a night of clear soft moonlight the people hear the clatter of many hoofs, the jingling of bridles, and the sound of laughter and sweet music coming sweetly down the wind, they whisper one to another: "'Tis the Fairy Folks' Raid", or "Here come the Riders of the Shee".

The Fairy Queen, who rides in front, is gowned in grass-green silk, and wears over her shoulders a mantle of green velvet adorned with silver spangles. She is of great beauty. Her eyes are like wood violets, her teeth like pearls, her brow and neck are swan-white, and her cheeks bloom like ripe apples. Her long clustering hair of rich auburn gold which falls over her shoulders and down her back, is bound round about with a snood that glints with star-like gems, and there is one great flashing jewel above her brow. On each lock of her horse's mane hang sweet-toned silver bells that tinkle merrily as she rides on.

The riders who follow her in couples are likewise clad in green, and wear little red caps bright as the flaming poppies in waving fields of yellow barley. Their horses' manes are hung with silver whistles upon which the soft winds play. Some fairies twang harps of gold, some make sweet music on oaten pipes, and some sing with birdlike voices in the moonlight. When song and music cease, they chat and laugh merrily as they ride on their way. Over hills and down glens they go, but no hoof-mark is left by their horses. So lightly do the little white creatures trot that not a grass blade is broken by their tread, nor is the honey-dew spilled from blue harebells and yellow buttercups. Sometimes the fairies ride over tree-tops or through the air on eddies of western wind. The Riders of the Shee always come from the west.

When the Summer Fairy Raid is coming, the people hang branches of rowan over their doors and round their rooms, and when the Winter Raid is coming they hang up holly and mistletoe as protection from attack; for sometimes the fairies steal pretty children while they lie fast asleep, and carry them off to Fairyland, and sometimes they lure away pipers and bards, and women who have sweet singing voices.

Once there was a great bard who was called Thomas the Rhymer. He lived at Ercildoune (Earlston), in Berwickshire, during the thirteenth century. It is told that he vanished for seven years, and that when he reappeared he had the gift of prophecy. Because he was able to foretell events, he was given the name of True Thomas.

All through Scotland, from the Cheviot Hills to the Pentland Firth, the story of Thomas the Rhymer has long been known.

During his seven years' absence from home be is said to have dwelt in fairyland. One evening, so runs the tale, he was walking alone on the banks of Leader Water when he saw riding towards him the Fairy Queen on her milk-white steed, the silver bells tinkling on its mane, and the silver bridle jingling sweet and clear. He was amazed at her beauty, and thinking she was the Queen of Heaven, bared his head and knelt before her as she dismounted, saying: "All hail, mighty Queen of Heaven! I have never before seen your equal."

Said the green-clad lady: "Ah! Thomas, you have named me wrongly. I am the Queen of Fairyland, and have come to visit you."

"What seek you with me?" Thomas asked.

Said the Fairy Queen: "You must hasten at once to Fairyland, and serve me there for seven years."

Then she laid a spell upon him, and he had to obey her will. She mounted her milk-white steed and Thomas mounted behind her, and they rode off together. They crossed the Leader Water, and the horse went swifter than the wind over hill and dale until a great wide desert was reached. No house nor human being could be seen anywhere. East and west, north and south, the level desert stretched as far as eye could see. They rode on and on until at length the Fairy Queen spoke, and said: "Dismount, O Thomas, and I shall show you three wonders."

Thomas dismounted and the Fairy Queen dismounted also. Said she: "Look, yonder is a narrow road full of thorns and briers. That is the path to Heaven. Yonder is a broad highway which runs across a lily lea. That is the path of wickedness. Yonder is another road. It twines round the hill-side towards the west. That is the way to Fairyland, and you and I must ride thither."

Again she mounted her milk-white steed and Thomas mounted behind. They rode on and on, crossing many rivers. Nor sun or moon could be seen nor any stars, and in the silence and thick darkness they heard the deep voice of the roaring sea.

At length a light appeared in front of them, which grew larger and brighter as they rode on. Then Thomas saw a beautiful country. The horse halted and he found himself in the midst of a green garden. When they had dismounted, the Fairy Queen plucked an apple and gave it to, Thomas, saying: "This is your reward for coming with me. After you have eaten of it you will have power to speak truly of coming events, and men will know you as 'True Thomas'."

Thomas ate the apple and then followed the queen to her palace. He was given clothing of green silk and shoes of green velvet, and he dwelt among the fairies for seven years. The time passed so quickly that the seven years seemed no longer than seven hours.

After his return to Ercildoune, where he lived in a castle, Thomas made many songs and ballads and pronounced in rhyme many prophecies. He travelled up and down the country, and wherever he went he foretold events, some of which took place while yet he lived among men, but others did not happen until long years afterwards. There are still some prophecies which are as yet unfulfilled.

It is said that when Thomas was an old man the Fairy Queen returned for him. One day, as he stood chatting with knights and ladies, she rode from the river-side and called: "True Thomas, your time has come."

Thomas cried to his friends: "Farewell, all of you, I shall return no more." Then he mounted the milk-white steed behind the Fairy Queen, and galloped across the ford. Several knights leapt into their saddles and followed the Rider of the Shee, but when they reached the opposite bank of the river they could see naught of Thomas and the Fairy Queen.

It is said that Thomas still dwells in Fairyland, and that he goes about among the Riders of the Shee when they come forth at the beginning of each summer. Those who have seen him ride past tell that he looks very old, and that his hair and long beard are white as driven snow. At other times he goes about invisible, except when he attends a market to buy horses for a fairy army which is to take part in a great battle. He drives the horses to Fairyland and keeps them there. When he has collected a suffi-cient number, it is told, he will return again to wage war against the invaders of his country, whom he will defeat on the banks of the Clyde.

Thomas wanders far and wide through Scotland. He has been seen, folks have told, riding out of a fairy dwelling below Eildon Hills, from another fairy dwelling below Dumbuck Hill, near Dumbarton, and from a third fairy dwelling below the boat-shaped mound of Tom-na-hurich at Inverness.

Once a man who climbed Dumbuck Hill came to an open door and entered through it. In a dim chamber he saw a little old man resting on his elbow, who spoke to him and said: "Has the time come?"

The man was stricken with fear and fled away. When he pressed through the doorway, the door shut behind him, and turf closed over it.

Another story about Thomas is told at Inverness. Two fiddlers, named Farquhar Grant and Thomas Cumming, natives of Strathspey, who lived over three hundred years ago, once visited Inverness during the Christmas season. They hoped to earn money by their music, and as soon as they arrived in the town began to show their skill in the streets. Although they had great fame as fiddlers in Strathspey, they found that the townspeople took little notice of them. When night fell, they had not collected enough money to buy food for supper and to pay for a night's lodging. They stopped playing and went, with their fiddles under their right arms, towards the wooden bridge that then crossed the River Ness.

Just as they were about to walk over the bridge they saw a little old man coming towards them in the dusk. His beard was very long and very white, but although his back was bent his step was easy and light. He stopped in front of the fiddlers, and, much to their surprise, hailed them by their names saying: "How fares it with you, my merry fiddlers?"

"Badly, badly!" answered Grant.

"Very badly indeed!" Cumming said.

"Come with me," said the old man. "I have need of fiddlers to-night, and will reward you well. A great ball is to be held in my castle, and there are no musicians."

Grant and Cumming were glad to get the chance of earning money by playing their fiddles and said they would go. "Then follow me and make haste," said the old man. The fiddlers followed him across the wooden bridge and across the darkening moor beyond. He walked with rapid strides, and sometimes the fiddlers had to break into a run to keep up with him. Now and again that strange, nimble old man would turn round and cry: "Are you coming, my merry fiddlers?"

"We are doing our best," Grant would answer, while Cumming muttered: "By my faith, old man, but you walk quickly!"

"Make haste, Grant; make haste, Cumming, the old man would then exclaim; "my guests will be growing impatient."

In time they reached the big boat-shaped mound called Tom-na-hurich, and the old man began to climb it. The fiddlers followed at a short distance. Then he stopped suddenly and stamped the ground three times with his right foot. A door opened and a bright light streamed forth.

"Here is my castle, Cumming; here is my castle, Grant," exclaimed the old man, who was no other than Thomas the Rhymer. "Come within and make merry."

The fiddlers paused for a moment at the open door, but Thomas the Rhymer drew from his belt a purse of gold and made it jingle. "This purse holds your wages," he told them. "First you will get your share of the feast, then you will give us fine music."

As the fiddlers were as hungry as they were poor, they could not resist the offer made to them, and entered the fairy castle. As soon as they entered, the door was shut behind them.

They found themselves in a great hall, which was filled with brilliant light. Tables were spread with all kinds of food, and guests sat round them eating and chatting and laughing merrily.

Thomas led the fiddlers to a side table, and two graceful maidens clad in green came forward with dishes of food and bottles of wine, and said: "Eat and drink to your hearts' content, Farquhar Grant and Thomas Cumming—Farquhar o'Feshie and Thomas o' Tom-an-Torran. You are welcome here to-night."

The fiddlers wondered greatly that the maidens knew not only their personal names but even the names of their homes. They began to eat, and, no matter how much they ate, the food on the table did not seem to grow less. They poured out wine, but they could not empty the bottles.

Said Cumming: "This is a feast indeed."

Said Grant: "There was never such a feast in Strathspey."

When the feast was ended the fiddlers were led to the ballroom, and there they began to play merry music for the gayest and brightest and happiest dancers they ever saw before. They played reels and jigs and strathspeys, and yet never grew weary. The dancers praised their music, and fair girls brought them fruit and wine at the end of each dance. If the guests were happy, the musicians were happier still, and they were sorry to find at length that the ball was coming to an end. How long it had lasted they could not tell. When the dancers began to go away they were still unwearied and willing to go on playing.

Thomas the Rhymer entered the ballroom, and spoke to the fiddlers, saying: "You have done well, my merry men. I will lead you to the door, and pay you for your fine music."

The fiddlers were sorry to go away. At the door Thomas the Rhymer divided the purse of gold between them, and asked: "Are you satisfied?"

"Satisfied!" Cumming repeated. "Oh, yes, for you and your guests have been very kind!"

"We should gladly come back again," Grant said.

When they had left the castle the fiddlers found that it was bright day. The sun shone from an unclouded sky, and the air was warm. As they walked on they were surprised to see fields of ripe corn, which was a strange sight at the Christmas season. Then they came to the riverside, and found instead of a wooden bridge a new stone bridge with seven arches.

"This stone bridge was not here last night," Cumming said.

"Not that I saw," said Grant.

When they crossed the bridge they found that the town of Inverness had changed greatly. Many new houses had been built; there were even new streets. The people they saw moving about wore strange clothing. One spoke to the fiddlers, and asked: "Who are you, and whence come you?"

They told him their names, and said that on the previous night they had played their fiddles at a great ball in a castle near the town.

The man smiled. Then Farquhar said: "The bridge we crossed over last evening was made of wood. Now you have a bridge of stone. Have the fairies built it for you?"

The man laughed, and exclaimed, as he turned away: "You are mad. The stone bridge was built before I was born."

Boys began to collect round the fiddlers. They jeered at their clothing, and cried: "Go back to the madhouse you have escaped from."

The fiddlers hastened out of the town, and took the road which leads to Strathspey. Men who passed them stopped and looked back, but they spoke to no one, and scarcely spoke, indeed, to one another.

Darkness came on, and they crept into an empty, half-ruined house by the wayside and slept there. How long they slept they knew not, but when they came out again they saw that the harvesting had begun. Fields were partly cut, but no workers could be seen in them, although the sun was already high in the heavens. They drank water from a well, and went on their way, until at length they reached their native village. They entered it joyfully, but were unable to find their homes. There, too, new houses had been built, and strange faces were seen. They heard a bell ringing, and then knew it was Sabbath day, and they walked towards the church. A man spoke to them near the gate of the churchyard and said: "You are strangers here."

"No, indeed, we are not strangers," Grant assured him. "This is our native village."

"You must have left it long ago," said the man, "for I have lived here all my life, and I do not know you."

Then Grant told his name and that of his companion, and the names of their fathers and mothers. "We are fine fiddlers," he added; "our equal is not to be found north of the Grampians."

Said the man: "Ah! you are the two men my grandfather used to speak of. He never saw you, but he heard his father tell that you had been decoyed by Thomas the Rhymer, who took you to Tom-na-hurich. Your friends mourned for you greatly, but now you are quite forgotten, for it is fully a hundred years since you went away from here."

The fiddlers thought that the man was mocking them, and turned their backs upon him. They went into the churchyard, and began to read the names on the gravestones. They saw stones erected to their wives and children, and to their children's children, and gazed on them with amazement, taking no notice of the people who passed by to the church door.

At length they entered the church hand in hand, with their fiddles under their arms. They stood for a brief space at the doorway, gazing at the congregation, but were unable to recognise a single face among the people who looked round at them.

The minister was in the pulpit. He had been told who the strangers were, and, after gazing for a moment in silence, he began to pray. No sooner did he do so than the two fiddlers crumbled into dust.

Such is the story of the two fiddlers who spent a hundred years in a fairy dwelling, thinking they had played music there for but a single night.

Taken from *Wonder Tales from Scottish Myth and Legend* by Donald Alexander Mackenzie, Frederick A Stokes Co., New York. [1917] Scanned at sacred-texts.com, February, 2004. John Bruno Hare, redactor. This text is in the public domain. These files may be used for any non-commercial purpose, provided this notice of attribution is left intact.

There is strong, though not conclusive, archaeological evidence to indicate that what we call shamanism was once practised in this land of ours, the land that gave birth to Thomas the Rhymer, and others who have journeyed both out of this reality and back again to tell their tales:

[In Upton Lovell in Wiltshire there is a round barrow covering] an adult male skeleton with rows of thin, perforated bones about his neck, thighs and feet. They had almost certainly hung in fringes from his clothes With him were fine stone axe-heads, boars' tusks, white flints and pebbles of a stone not found in the area. A similar mound at Youlgreave, Derbyshire, held a man with the teeth of a dog and a horse under his head and a round bronze amulet on his chest. With him were an ace, quartz pebbles and a piece of porphyry. The ashes of another burial from a lost barrow near Stonehenge were mixed with four stained rectangular bronze tablets, one plain and the others incised with a cross or a star or a lozenge (Bronze Age tarot cards?). All these suggest the presence not so much of a priesthood as of shamans or medicine people, familiar in the tribal peoples of the modern world (Hutton, 1993, p.109).

We also know from Roman accounts that among the Gallic tribes there was a belief in some kind of afterlife, and their Otherworld might well have been sub-divided into different planes. One of these planes could have been a Land of the Dead that their shamans or medicine people would have been able to journey to.

Caesar, Strabo, Diodorus Siculus, Pomponius Mela, Lucan and Ammianus Marcellinus all mention the belief of the Gallic Tribes that the soul survived death. Caesar and Pomponius were reminded of the Greek doctrine of Pythagoras, whereby souls were reborn in new bodies, but were shocked by the very literal way in which the people of Gaul believed that the human being transcended the grave (Hutton, 1993, p.183).

In most of the early Irish and some of the early Welsh tales, there is a divine Otherworld which is a superlative version of the mortal one. Its people enjoy eternal life in the sense that they do not grow old or fall sick, but they can, apparently, be killed ... This Otherworld can be entered from the human one by certain doors concealed in mounds, or islands, or hills, or in the floors of lakes or the bed of the sea (ibid. p.184)

And as to how the Land of the Dead might have been accessed, in view of the way ships feature as vessels for bodies in both literary sources and in cemeteries, this could well have been by crossing water, by means of a bridge or in a boat of some kind:

Ships feature as receptacles for bodies in several literary sources for German and Scandinavian society: in *Beowulf*, in Viking sagas and in an Arab traveller's account of the Swedish settlers in Russia. The prominence of vessels in the rock art of the Scandinavian Bronze Age ... and the beliefs which inspired these pictures may have carried over into the period represented by the literature (Hutton, 1993, p.177).

[The wonderful treasure discovered in Sutton Hoo in 1938] was piled inside a clinker-built ship 90 feet long beneath an oval mound, and probably accompanied a body which had completely vanished because of the acidic soil. All circumstances combine to date the deposit to the 620s or 630s, and the most likely person to have occupied the grave would have been Raedwald, king of East Anglia (ibid. pp.277-278).

As to whether Thomas was a shaman or not, all we can do is to speculate, but from the limited information that is available to us, it seems that it could well have been the case.

Many of the Indian tribes of North America believed that their Medicine Men were endowed with supernatural attributes, as it was not possible for all and sundry to obtain such distinction. Far from it. Anyone desirous of attaining that dignity had to receive tuition from the older adepts in the art, and also to undergo the most severe trials. These took place in the depths of the forest. The novice had to fast until he almost succumbed from starvation, and had to wound and otherwise torture himself in various ways. The effect of all this was to induce dreams in which spirits figured, and to cause him to believe that they gave him various messages. After passing all the tests successfully he was initiated into the mysteries of the profession, and thus became a fully-fledged Medicine Man (Porteous, 2002, pp.42-43).

Thomas Rhymer received his tuition from the Queen of Elfland herself, who was also responsible for setting the trials he had to undergo. Only then was he considered to be fully trained and allowed to practise his art, until the time came for him to be called away again.

Reference

Hutton, R. (1993) *The Pagan Religions of the Ancient British Isles: Their Nature and Legacy*, Oxford: Blackwell Publishing.

Porteous, A. (2002) *The Forest in Folklore and Mythology*, Mineola, New York: Dover Publications, Inc. (Originally published by the Macmillan Company, New York, in 1928).

The Girl and the Skull

Once upon a time there was an old man and his wife. They were three in the family. Their daughter was the third. The daughter was a girl unmarried, without a husband. This daughter had a separate sleeping-room. They had two sleeping-rooms. That of the daughter was separate. She was sleeping all by herself. The parents were sleeping together.

Once upon a time the (young) woman went out and was walking about there. Then she found a bare skull lying in the wilderness. She put it into one leg of her breeches and took it home, this human skull. She carried it into her sleeping-room. There she concealed it. She made a cap, puckered (along the border). With that cap she covered the skull. Then every evening, as soon as the sleeping-rooms had been put in order, the woman set the skull near the rear wall, then she laughed at it. And that bare skull also laughed a little, "Hm!" Her mother heard it, and said, "What may she be laughing at, this one?" — "I am laughing only at a cap, newly made and adorned." Thus she deceived her mother. Then every time when she awoke in the morning, she put the skull in the bottom of the bag, lest they should find it.

Once, when the girl was again walking outside, her mother took out the contents of her daughter's bag-pillow. She was looking for something, and therefore searched in the bag-pillow of her daughter. Suddenly she caught that skull by the mouth and took it out. She was startled. "Oh, oh, oh, horror! horror! What has become of our daughter? How very strange! Our [quite] unmarried daughter has become a ke´le̦, she has become an abomination, an object of fear. Oh, wonder! what is she now? Not a human being. In truth, she is a ke´le̦."

The father presently said, "Oh, let us leave! No need of her. You speak to her to-morrow, and invite her to a walk outside with you."

Just as before (the mother) filled her bag-pillow and closed it in the same manner. The girl came back, it grew dark, and they lay down to sleep. Again she set (the skull) in the evening before herself, and laughed at it, "Hi, hi!" And the other answered, "Hm!"

"How wonderful you are, O woman! Why are you laughing so, being alone, quite   alone in your sleeping-room?" — "No, indeed! I am only laughing at a cap, newly made and adorned."

On the next day the mother said, "Let us go and fetch fuel." They gathered fuel, cut wood, and broke off (branches of) bushes. Then the mother said, "The wood-binding is too short. I will go and get some more. Surely, I shall be back soon." — "No, indeed, I will go." — "No, I." — "Ah, well, go and get it."

So the mother went home. When she came home, her husband had broken camp and loaded a boat. He loaded the tent on the boat. They were setting off for the opposite shore. They left their daughter and cast her off. When they had almost finished, the girl could not wait any longer; therefore she went to look. She was moving along the steep river-bank when she saw that boat loaded, and (her father's) work finished. Oh, she ran on and rushed to them. Just as she came, they went aboard and her father pushed off. The girl held on to the steering-paddle, but her father struck her with a paddle on the wrist. So she let go of the steering-paddle. They left her, and set off far away for the other shore.

The daughter was left quite alone at the camp-site. Even though a house had   been there, there was now nothing at all, no house. Therefore she began to weep, and put that bare skull outside. Then she pushed it with her foot, and said, weeping, "This one is the cause of (it) all. What has he done, the bad one? They have left me, they have cast me off. Oh, dear!"

Then the bare skull began to speak, "You make me suffer, indeed. Do not push   me with your foot. Better let me go and procure a body for myself, only do not push me so. Go and make

73

a wood-pile, make a fire, then throw me into the flames." — "Oh, all right! Then, however, I shall quite alone. I can talk with you at least." — "Obey me, indeed. You are suffering, quite vainly we suffer together. I shall procure a body for myself."

Oh, she made a fire. It blazed up. Then the skull spoke to her again, and said, "Well, now, throw me into the fire! Then stay with head drawn back into the collar of your dress, in this manner, and do not look up. Indeed, no matter who may look upon you, or what voices you may hear, do not look up!"

She obeyed, threw (the skull) into the fire, then staid with head drawn back and bent down. Thus she remained. Then the fire blazed up with a noise for a long time. Then it went out. She remained with her head bent down, then she began to hear a noise, a clattering of runners; then also, "Oh, oh, oh, oh, oh, oh!" from a herd; loud voices, "Ah, ah, ah; ah, ah, ah!" and whistling. Then a caravan clattered by, still she continued to sit with head bent down. The clattering came nearer, and the cries, "Waġo', yaġo'!" Then a man called her from the front. "Well, there, what are you doing? Oh, she looked up. A large caravan was coming. The herd was quite big. The man, her husband, was standing in front of her, clad in a shirt made of thin furs, in the best of skins.

They built a camp, and put up the tent. He was quite rich in reindeer. Then, in truth, she began to feel quite well.

In the beginning of the cold, early in the fall, (the parents of the woman) saw smoke rising. "Come, say, what settlement have we noticed just now? Come, let us go and visit it." They crossed with a boat, her parents, the father with the mother, "Oh, sit down in the outer tent. I shall cook some food for you." She prepared for cooking, and filled the kettle with meat and fat.

While she was cooking, she broke some thigh-bones to extract the marrow. When the meal was finished, she gave them the marrow (with the bone splinters). "Eat this marrow!" They ate the marrow, but the thigh-bone splinters stuck in their throats and pierced them. Thus she killed them, and they died. Finished.

I have killed the wind.

Told by Ṛịke'wg̣i, a Maritime Chukchee man, at Mariinsky Post, in October, 1900, and taken from Bogoras, W. (1910) *Chukchee Mythology*, Leiden & New York. In *The Jessup North Pacific Expedition* Edited by Franz Boas. Memoir of the American Museum of Natural History New York, Volume VIII

Among the Chukchee, records Bogoras, the soul is called *uvi'rit*, or sometimes *uvê'kkirgin*, both words coming from the same root meaning "body." The seat of the soul is believed to lie in the heart or the liver and both animals and plants have souls as well as people. As well as the soul pertaining to the whole body, people are believed to have several other souls. For example:

There are special "limb-souls" for the hands and feet. Occasionally these latter may be lost, [and] then the corresponding limb begins to ache and gradually withers. The Chukchee call a man whose nose is easily frostbitten "short of souls" (*uviri'tkilin*), meaning that some part of his vital force must have left his body unawares. The "limb-souls" stay on the spot where they were lost. A shaman, however, can call them to himself, and they become his "assistant spirits" (*ya'nřa-ka'lat*). The "souls" are very small. When passing by, the produce a sound like the humming of a bee of the droning of a beetle (Bogoras, 1910, pp.332-33).

If one or all of the "souls" are stolen, then a person can become sick and die. The shaman, however, is believed to be able to find and restore a missing "soul," which often assumes the shape of a black beetle. When put on the body of the patient, it will crawl all over his head, trying to find a hole into which to slip. Then the shaman will open the skull, and put the beetle in its proper place ... If the shaman fails to find the "soul," he can blow into the person a part of his own spirit to become a "soul;" or he may give him one of his "assistant *ke'let*" [spirits] to replace the missing "soul" (Bogoras, 1910, p.333).

As for the Chukchee "ventriloquists", we are informed they display great skill,

> *and could with credit to themselves carry on a contest with the best artists of the kind of civilized countries. The "separate voices" of their calling come from all sides of the room, changing their place to the complete illusion of their listeners. Some voices are at first faint, as if coming from afar; as they gradually approach, they increase in volume, and at last they rush into the room, pass through it and out, decreasing, and dying away in the remote distance. Other voices come from above, pass through the room and seem to go underground, where they are heard as if from the depths of the earth. Tricks of this kind are played also with the voices of animals and birds, and even with the howling of the tempest, producing a most weird effect* (Bogoras, 1910, p.435).

Though Bogoras calls the Chukchee shamans ventriloquists and refers to the tricks they perform, this does not necessarily have to be taken as a derogatory reference. After all, the shaman's effectiveness is dependent on his ability to sweep the audience along with the power of his performance. Props and symbols are used by the shaman both to represent the psychic experience he undergoes and also to affect the experience of those taking part in the proceedings (see Vitebsky, 2001, p.52). Stone makes a similar point: "Everyone likes a good show and many shamans give full value for money, with impressive singing, drumming and dancing, conjuring tricks, and plenty of eye-rolling and melodramatic grimacing" (Stone, 2003, p.66). Indeed, the use of trickery can have a significant part to play in the shamanic séance. So more important perhaps than whether the shaman performs an ecstatic (in a trance state), imitative, or demonstrative ritual of a séance, is whether what he / she does is effective or not.

Sheol is the Hebrew name for the underworld, the realm of the dead located deep below the earth. It is a place of no return (Job 16:22), a place of captivity with gates (Is. 38:10) and bars (Jonah 2:6). The Underworld in other traditions, however, is more accessible, with there being a two-way bridge in place between this world and the next.

Incantation to bring back the Dying

When a man has (just) died, (another person) goes into the open, while (the dead [person]) is still lying in the inner room. That man goes out and talks to the Morning Dawn, to the Upper Being. He says, "Oh, my mind is uncertain! Enough! Whom (else) may I ask (for help)? You are most fit. Oh, give me your dog! I will also use it as a dog myself. I am sorrowful for my child. It has gone away to a far-off (place). Therefore let me use that (dog) for (my) assistant."

He makes (a motion) with his left hand, as if receiving that dog (from somewhere). Then he (comes back and) blows into the ear of the dead person, and howls (like a dog), "Uu, uu!" thus.

Then this dog starts on, pursuing the dead man, [who has gone away.] It follows him, howling and barking, "Haw, haw, haw!" It passes ahead of him, and meets him (on the road with fierce) barking. It snaps at him (while he is) going, and intercepts his path in every direction. At last it makes him come back from his long journey. He must enter the body and put it on again. Then he begins to breathe, and (gradually) improves. And so he, though a real dead (one), revives again.

Told by Ṛike'wg̣i, a Maritime Chukchee man, at Mariinsky Post, in October, 1900, and taken from Bogoras, W. (1910) *Chukchee Mythology*, Leiden & New York. In *The Jessup North Pacific Expedition* Edited by Franz Boas. Memoir of the American Museum of Natural History New York, Volume VIII.

References

Bogoras, W. (1910) *Publications of the Jessup North Pacific Expedition 1904-1909*, Volume VII, *The Chukchee*, Leiden: E.J. Brill Ltd.

Stone, A. (2003) *Explore Shamanism*, UK: Loughborough: Heart of Albion Press.

Vitebsky, P. (2001) *The Shaman*, London: Duncan Baird (first published in Great Britain in 1995 by Macmillan Reference Books).

The Story of the Man who did not wish to Die

Long, long ago there lived a man called Sentaro. His surname meant "Millionaire," but although he was not so rich as all that, he was still very far removed from being poor. He had inherited a small fortune from his father and lived on this, spending his time carelessly, without any serious thoughts of work, till he was about thirty-two years of age.

One day, without any reason whatsoever, the thought of death and sickness came to him. The idea of falling ill or dying made him very wretched.

"I should like to live," he said to himself, "till I am five or six hundred years old at least, free from all sickness. The ordinary span of a man's life is very short."

He wondered whether it were possible, by living simply and frugally henceforth, to prolong his life as long as he wished.

He knew there were many stories in ancient history of emperors who had lived a thousand years, and there was a Princess of Yamato, who, it was said, lived to the age of five hundred. This was the latest story of a very long life record.

Sentaro had often heard the tale of the Chinese King named Shin-no-Shiko. He was one of the most able and powerful rulers in Chinese history. He built all the large palaces, and also the famous Great Wall of China. He had everything in the world he could wish for, but in spite of all his happiness and the luxury and the splendour of his Court, the wisdom of his councillors and the glory of his reign, he was miserable because he knew that one day he must die and leave it all.

When Shin-no-Shiko went to bed at night, when he rose in the morning, as he went through his day, the thought of death was always with him. He could not get away from it. Ah—if only he could find the "Elixir of Life," he would be happy.

The Emperor at last called a meeting of his courtiers and asked them all if they could not find for him the "Elixir of Life" of which he had so often read and heard.

One old courtier, Jofuku by name, said that far away across the seas there was a country called Horaizan, and that certain hermits lived there who possessed the secret of the "Elixir of Life." Whoever drank of this wonderful draught lived forever.

The Emperor ordered Jofuku to set out for the land of Horaizan, to find the hermits, and to bring him back a phial of the magic elixir. He gave Jofuku one of his best junks, fitted it out for him, and loaded it with great quantities of treasures and precious stones for Jofuku to take as presents to the hermits.

Jofuku sailed for the land of Horaizan, but he never returned to the waiting Emperor; but ever since that time Mount Fuji has been said to be the fabled Horaizan and the home of hermits who had the secret of the elixir, and Jofuku has been worshipped as their patron god.

Now Sentaro determined to set out to find the hermits, and if he could, to become one, so that he might obtain the water of perpetual life. He remembered that as a child he had been told that not only did these hermits live on Mount Fuji, but that they were said to inhabit all the very high peaks.

So he left his old home to the care of his relatives, and started out on his quest. He travelled through all the mountainous regions of the land, climbing to the tops of the highest peaks, but never a hermit did he find.

At last, after wandering in an unknown region for many days, he met a hunter.

"Can you tell me," asked Sentaro, "where the hermits live who have the Elixir of Life?"

"No." said the hunter; "I can't tell you where such hermits live, but there is a notorious robber living in these parts. It is said that he is chief of a band of two hundred followers."

This odd answer irritated Sentaro very much, and he thought

how foolish it was to waste more time in looking for the hermits in this way, so he decided to go at once to the shrine of Jofuku, who is worshipped as the patron god of the hermits in the south of Japan.

Sentaro reached the shrine and prayed for seven days, entreating Jofuku to show him the way to a hermit who could give him what he wanted so much to find.

At midnight of the seventh day, as Sentaro knelt in the temple, the door of the innermost shrine flew open, and Jofuku appeared in a luminous cloud, and calling to Sentaro to come nearer, spoke thus:

"Your desire is a very selfish one and cannot be easily granted. You think that you would like to become a hermit so as to find the Elixir of Life. Do you know how hard a hermit's life is? A hermit is only allowed to eat fruit and berries and the bark of pine trees; a hermit must cut himself off from the world so that his heart may become as pure as gold and free from every earthly desire. Gradually after following these strict rules, the hermit ceases to feel hunger or cold or heat, and his body becomes so light that he can ride on a crane or a carp, and can walk on water without getting his feet wet."

"You, Sentaro, are fond of good living and of every comfort. You are not even like an ordinary man, for you are exceptionally idle, and more sensitive to heat and cold than most people. You would never be able to go barefoot or to wear only one thin dress in the winter time! Do you think that you would ever have the patience or the endurance to live a hermit's life?"

"In answer to your prayer, however, I will help you in another way. I will send you to the country of Perpetual Life, where death never comes—where the people live forever!"

Saying this, Jofuku put into Sentaro's hand a little crane made of paper, telling him to sit on its back and it would carry him there.

Sentaro obeyed wonderingly. The crane grew large enough

for him to ride on it with comfort. It then spread its wings, rose high in the air, and flew away over the mountains right out to sea.

Sentaro was at first quite frightened; but by degrees he grew accustomed to the swift flight through the air. On and on they went for thousands of miles. The bird never stopped for rest or food, but as it was a paper bird it doubtless did not require any nourishment, and strange to say, neither did Sentaro.

After several days they reached an island. The crane flew some distance inland and then alighted.

As soon as Sentaro got down from the bird's back, the crane folded up of its own accord and flew into his pocket.

Now Sentaro began to look about him wonderingly, curious to see what the country of Perpetual Life was like. He walked first round about the country and then through the town. Everything was, of course, quite strange, and different from his own land. But both the land and the people seemed prosperous, so he decided that it would be good for him to stay there and took up lodgings at one of the hotels.

The proprietor was a kind man, and when Sentaro told him that he was a stranger and had come to live there, he promised to arrange everything that was necessary with the governor of the city concerning Sentaro's sojourn there. He even found a house for his guest, and in this way Sentaro obtained his great wish and became a resident in the country of Perpetual Life.

Within the memory of all the islanders no man had ever died there, and sickness was a thing unknown. Priests had come over from India and China and told them of a beautiful country called Paradise, where happiness and bliss and contentment fill all men's hearts, but its gates could only be reached by dying. This tradition was handed down for ages from generation to generation—but none knew exactly what death was except that it led to Paradise.

Quite unlike Sentaro and other ordinary people, instead of having a great dread of death, they all, both rich and poor, longed for it as something good and desirable. They were all tired of their long, long lives, and longed to go to the happy land of contentment called Paradise of which the priests had told them centuries ago.

All this Sentaro soon found out by talking to the islanders. He found himself, according to his ideas, in the land of Topsyturvydom. Everything was upside down. He had wished to escape from dying. He had come to the land of Perpetual Life with great relief and joy, only to find that the inhabitants themselves, doomed never to die, would consider it bliss to find death.

What he had hitherto considered poison these people ate as good food, and all the things to which he had been accustomed as food they rejected. Whenever any merchants from other countries arrived, the rich people rushed to them eager to buy poisons. These they swallowed eagerly, hoping for death to come so that they might go to Paradise.

But what were deadly poisons in other lands were without effect in this strange place, and people who swallowed them with the hope of dying, only found that in a short time they felt better in health instead of worse.

Vainly they tried to imagine what death could be like. The wealthy would have given all their money and all their goods if they could but shorten their lives to two or three hundred years even. Without any change to live on forever seemed to this people wearisome and sad.

In the chemist shops there was a drug which was in constant demand, because after using it for a hundred years, it was supposed to turn the hair slightly gray and to bring about disorders of the stomach.

Sentaro was astonished to find that the poisonous globe-fish was served up in restaurants as a delectable dish, and hawkers in the streets went about selling sauces made of Spanish flies. He never saw any one ill after eating these horrible things, nor did he ever see any one with as much as a cold.

Sentaro was delighted. He said to himself that he would never grow tired of living, and that he considered it profane to wish for death. He was the only happy man on the island. For his part he wished to live thousands of years and to enjoy life. He set himself up in business, and for the present never even dreamed of going back to his native land.

As years went by, however, things did not go as smoothly as at first. He had heavy losses in business, and several times some affairs went wrong with his neighbours. This caused him great annoyance.

Time passed like the flight of an arrow for him, for he was busy from morning till night. Three hundred years went by in this monotonous way, and then at last he began to grow tired of life in this country, and he longed to see his own land and his old home. However long he lived here, life would always be the game, so was it not foolish and wearisome to stay on here forever?

Sentaro, in his wish to escape from the country of Perpetual Life, recollected Jofuku, who had helped him before when he was wishing to escape from death—and he prayed to the saint to bring him back to his own land again.

No sooner did he pray than the paper crane popped out of his pocket. Sentaro was amazed to see that it had remained undamaged after all these years. Once more the bird grew and grew till it was large enough for him to mount it. As he did so, the bird spread its wings and flew, swiftly out across the sea in the direction of Japan.

Such was the wilfulness of the man's nature that he looked back and regretted all he had left behind. He tried to stop the bird in vain. The crane held on its way for thousands of miles across the ocean.

Then a storm came on, and the wonderful paper crane got damp, crumpled up, and fell into the sea. Sentaro fell with it.

Very much frightened at the thought of being drowned, he cried out loudly to Jofuku to save him. He looked round, but there was no ship in sight. He swallowed a quantity of sea-water, which only increased his miserable plight. While he was thus struggling to keep himself afloat, he saw a monstrous shark swimming towards him. As it came nearer it opened its huge mouth ready to devour him. Sentaro was all but paralysed with fear now that he felt his end so near, and screamed out as loudly as ever he could to Jofuku to come and rescue him.

Lo, and behold, Sentaro was awakened by his own screams, to find that during his long prayer he had fallen asleep before the shrine, and that all his extraordinary and frightful adventures had been only a wild dream. He was in a cold perspiration with fright, and utterly bewildered.

Suddenly a bright light came towards him, and in the light stood a messenger. The messenger held a book in his hand, and spoke to Sentaro:

"I am sent to you by Jofuku, who in answer to your prayer, has permitted you in a dream to see the land of Perpetual Life. But you grew weary of living there, and begged to be allowed to return to your native land so that you might die. Jofuku, so that he might try you, allowed you to drop into the sea, and then sent a shark to swallow you up. Your desire for death was not real, for even at that moment you cried out loudly and shouted for help."

"It is also vain for you to wish to become a hermit, or to find the Elixir of Life. These things are not for such as you—a your life is not austere enough. It is best for you to go back to your paternal home, and to live a good and industrious life. Never neglect to keep the anniversaries of your ancestors, and make it your duty to provide for your children's future. Thus will you live to a good old age and be happy, but give up the vain desire to escape death, for no man can do that, and by this time you have surely found out that even when selfish desires are granted they do not bring happiness."

"In this book I give you there are many precepts good for you to know—if you study them, you will be guided in the way I have pointed out to you."

The angel disappeared as soon as he had finished speaking, and Sentaro took the lesson to heart. With the book in his hand he returned to his old home, and giving up all his old vain wishes, tried to live a good and useful life and to observe the lessons taught him in the book, and he and his house prospered henceforth.

Taken from The Project Gutenberg EBook of Japanese Fairy Tales, by Yei Theodora Ozaki. This eBook is for the use of anyone anywhere at no cost and with almost no restrictions whatsoever. You may copy it, give it away or re-use it under the terms of the Project Gutenberg License included with this eBook or online at www.gutenberg.net

Yei Theodora Ozaki was an early 20th century translator of Japanese short stories and fairy tales. According to "A Biographical Sketch" by Mrs. Hugh Fraser, included in the introductory material to *Warriors of old Japan, and other stories*, Ozaki came from an unusual background. She was the daughter of Baron Ozaki, one of the first Japanese men to study in the West, and Bathia Catherine Morrison, daughter of William Morrison, one of their teachers. Her parents separated after five years of marriage, and her mother retained custody of their three daughters until they became teenagers. At that time, Yei was sent to live in Japan with her father, which she enjoyed. Later she refused an arranged marriage, left her father's house, and became a teacher and secretary to earn money. Over the years, she travelled back and forth between Japan and Europe, as her employment and family duties took her, and lived in places as diverse as Italy and the drafty upper floor of a Buddhist temple. All this time, her letters were frequently misdelivered to the unrelated Japanese politician Yukio Ozaki, and his to her. In 1904, they finally met, and soon married.

The Wise Men of Gotham

All countries have had their special crop of fools, Boeotians among the Greeks, the people of Hums among the Persians, the Schildburgers in Germany, and so on. Gotham is the English representative. Nowadays, of course such jokes are not regarded as politically correct, and rightfully so, but given that Gotham is an imaginary place this can cause no offence to anyone. The source used by Joseph Jacobs for the tale that follows was the chap-book contained in Mr Hazlitt's *Shakespearian Jest Book,* vol. iii., which means it is basically the same story that would have been told in Elizabethan times:

There were two men of Gotham, and one of them was going to market to Nottingham to buy sheep, and the other came from the market, and they both met together upon Nottingham Bridge.

'Where are you going?' said the one who came from Nottingham.

'Marry,' said he that was going to Nottingham, 'I am going to buy sheep.'

'Buy sheep?' said the other. 'And which way will you bring them home?'

'Marry,' said the other, 'I will bring them over this bridge.'

'By Robin Hood,' said he that came from Nottingham, 'but thou shalt not.'

'By Maid Marion,' said he that was going thither, 'but I will.'

'You will not,' said the one.

'I will.'

Then they beat their staves against the ground one against the other, as if there had been a hundred sheep between them.

'Hold in,' said one; 'beware lest my sheep leap over the bridge.'

'I care not,' said the other; 'they shall not come this way.'

'But they shall,' said the other.

Then the other said: 'If that thou make much to do, I will put my fingers in thy mouth.'

'Will you?' said the other.

Now, as they were at their contention, another man of Gotham came from the market with a sack of meal upon a horse, and seeing and hearing his neighbours at strife about sheep, though there were none between them, said:

'Ah, fools! will you ever learn wisdom? Help me, and lay my sack upon my shoulders.'

They did so, and he went to the side of the bridge, unloosened the mouth of the sack, and shook all his meal out into the river.

'Now, neighbours,' he said, 'how much meal is there in my sack?'

'Marry,' said they, 'there is none at all.'

'Now, by my faith,' said he, 'even as much wit as is in your two heads to stir up strife about a thing you have not.'

Which was the wisest of these three persons? Judge for yourself!

Taken from Jacobs, J. (ed.) (1894) *More English Fairy Tales*, London, D. Nutt. Scanned and redacted by Phillip Brown. Additional proofing and formatting at sacred-texts.com by John B. Hare, April 2003. This text is in the public domain. These files may be used for any non-commercial purpose provided this notice of attribution is left intact.

* * *

While some of us struggle to stay on this side of the bridge, others cannot wait to cross over it. However, given that the crossing is inevitable in any case, it would seem to make more sense to focus on other matters.

Sweet William's Ghost

Sweet William's Ghost was collected by Francis James Child in 1868 and is listed as Child ballad number 77. A printed version appeared in Allan Ramsay's *The Tea-Table Miscellany* in 1740, and again in Thomas Percy's *Reliques of Ancient English Poetry* in 1765. Stories of type 365 from the Aarne-Thompson system of classifying folktales, of which this is an example, are about spectre bridegrooms who suddenly return to their fiancées, with it being unclear initially to their former partners as to whether they are still alive or dead.

The folk song exists in many forms but all versions recount a similar story and the reason for the bridegroom's crossing over is the same in each case too. The lover, usually named William or a variant, appears as a ghost to his love, usually Margaret or a variant. He asks her to release him from his promise to marry her. She may insist that he actually marry her, but he says that he is dead; she may insist that he kiss her, but he says that one kiss would kill her; she may insist on some information about the afterlife, and he tells her some of it; he may tell her that his promise to marry her is a hellhound that will destroy him if she does not free him. In the end she always releases him from his promise, although in some versions she then dies upon his grave. So it would seem that holding on to those who have crossed over does neither the bereaved person left behind nor the dead person any good once the allowed time for mourning is over.

In variant 77C of the ballad, presented below, the number three features prominently:

77C.11 'What three things are these, Sweet William,' she says,
      'That stands here at your head?'
77C.12 'What three things are these, Sweet William,' she says,

'That stands here at your side?'
77C.13 'What three things are these, Sweet William,' she says,
  'That stands here at your feet?'

Three is linked with the phases of the moon (waxing, full and waning), and with time (past, present and future). Pythagoras called three the perfect number in that it represented the beginning, the middle and the end, and he thus regarded it as a symbol of Deity. The importance of the number in the ballad could well be the result of the influence of Christianity and its use of the Trinity, but it also refers to the three stages in the cycle of life and adds to the universality of the story's appeal.

As for Variant 77F of the ballad, it is the number seven that is of significance as is made clear from the opening line: "WHEN seven years were come and gane".

Seven is a mystic or sacred number in many different traditions. Among the Babylonians and Egyptians, there were believed to be seven planets, and the alchemists recognised seven planets too. In the Old Testament there are seven days in creation, and for the Hebrews every seventh year was Sabbatical too. There are seven seven virtues, seven sins, seven ages in the life of man, seven wonders of the world, and the number seven repeatedly occurs in the *Apocalypse* as well. The Muslims talk of there being seven heavens, with the seventh being formed of divine light that is beyond the power of words to describe, and the Kabbalists also believe there are seven heavens–each arising above the other, with the seventh being the abode of God (Berman, 2008, p.122).

Seven was the Ancient Egyptian symbol of eternal life, and symbolises the dynamic perfection of a completed cycle. Seven conveys the fresh start after a cycle has been completed and of positive regeneration. Seven also occurs in countless Ancient Greek traditions and legends-the seven gates of Thebes, Niobe's seven sons and seven daughters, the seven strings of the lyre, the seven spheres, etc. There are seven emblems of the Buddha and seven primary chakras in the subtle energy system. The number seven was of special importance in the Zoroastrian religion too, where there were seven creations, seven regions of the world, seven Amesha Spenta (who became the seven archangels of Judaism), and so on.

In the Old Testament, the number seven symbolises God's perfection, His sovereignty and holiness. This is because God created earth in seven days, one seven-day week is a reminder of our creator, and also because God blessed the seventh day, making it holy (Exodus 20:8-11). It is also the number of days spent in mourning the dead. We know, for example, that the men of Jabesh-Gilead fasted for seven days after burying the bones of Saul and his sons (1 Sam. 31:13). Similarly, Jacob's family and Egyptian officials held a very great and sorrowful lamentation for seven days before burying him (Gen. 50:10).

The New Testament has the seven loaves and fishes; seven devils exorcised from Mary Magdalene; forgiveness seventy times seven. Also, Revelation has seven churches and many symbols are seven fold, usually because of the 7 angels (archangels). Luke's Gospel demonstrates that Jesus was predestined for greatness because great men occurred in multiples of seven generations starting from Adam, Enoch at 7, Abraham at 21, David at 35 and Jesus at 77, while Matthew demonstrates that Jesus was predestined for greatness because there were 14 generations from Josiah to Jesus, just as there had been 14 generations from David to Josiah and from Abraham to David (14 being 2 times 7). There were also seven heavens and the apocryphal *Ascension of Isaiah* had the Son descend into the lower world and then re-ascend to the seventh heaven.

What is of particular interest, in connection with variant 77F of the ballad presented below, is what we are told in the Old Testament—that Joshua led the Jewish People around the walls of Jericho seven times before the walls fell (Joshua 6:15), as seven indicates the number of years it takes to bring down the barrier between this world and the next in this version of the ballad too. It is also worth mentioning what we learn from Exodus 21:2 — which is a Jewish servant can regain his freedom after working for seven years, and in variant 77F after seven years it is the ghost who regains his freedom. Sheva, the Hebrew word for seven, comes from a root which means *complete,* and the number seven represents physical completion. In variant 77F, it is the period of mourning that is brought to completion in the ballad's resolution.

If ballad poetry finds much material in omen, portent, and curse, in the voices of birds, the cries of water-kelpie or banshee, in the speech of things inarticulate — if the natural world in which folk live thus goes hand in hand with the supernatural, inevitably it must communicate with the world of the dead. The few ghost-ballads of Britain ... ally themselves with a great group of Continental analogues, among which are some of the finest ballads in existence. A main theme of these is spirit visitation, the causes that disturb or call back departed souls being: the grief and tears of the living for the dead; the desire of the dead lover to receive back his troth, without which he cannot rest ; the lover's longing to carry his living sweetheart to the world of the dead; the sufferings of the living, especially of children ill-treated or neglected; hurt pride because the grave has been trodden by careless feet, or grazed by cattle; the desire to redress or expiate crimes committed in life; the desire like that of Dives in Hell to warn the living of the punishment that follows sin (Jewett, 1913, pp.17).

These ballads are, as Professor Child points out in his notes to Sweet William^ s Ghost, (vol. ii. p. 228), probably related to the tale of Helgi and Sigrun in the Elder Edda. The heroic traits of this magnificent epic fragment belong to a greater art than that of ballad-making, but the ballads have preserved the human pain and wistfulness, the wonder of the living at the touch of the dead, and the passionate yearning to share the fate of the beloved.

The teachings of the Church give, here and there, an ethical note to the ghost-lore, as in the remorseful craving of the spirit to return for the repairing of a wrong or for the warning of his kindred that they may escape his doom (Jewett, 1913, p.18).

Despite such lurid ecclesiastical colouring though, the conception of the dead as restless, earth-bound, haunters of the scenes they knew in life, clearly pre-dates Christianity.

"Sceptics will argue that it is impossible to eliminate from analysis the Christian influence on what sources there are available to us, such that we can never be certain in any one case that we are indeed dealing with beliefs that are authentically pagan. This view is now so widely held that we can in justice think of it as the prevailing orthodoxy" (Winterbourne, 2007, p.24).

Nevertheless, just because a task is difficult, in this case eliminating from analysis the Christian influence on what sources there are available to us, is no reason for us not to attempt to do so. If it was, then no progress would ever be made in any research that we might be involved in

References

Berman, M. (2008) *Divination and the Shamanic Story,* Newcastle: Cambridge Scholars Publishing.

Child, F. J. *Scottish and English Popular Ballads,* http://www.sacred-texts.com/neu/eng/child/ch77.htm

Jewett, S. (trans.) (1913) *Folk-Ballads of Southern Europe,* translated into English Verse by Sophie Jewett. New York and London: G. P. Putnam's Sons. http://www.archive.org/details/folkballadsofsouOOjewe

Winterbourne, A. (2007) *When The Norns Have Spoken: Time and Fate in Germanic Paganism,* Wales: Superscript.

77A: Sweet William's Ghost

77A.1   THERE came a ghost to Margret's door,
With many a grievous groan,
And ay he tirled at the pin,
But answer made she none.

77A.2   'Is that my father Philip,
Or is't my brother John?
Or is't my true-love, Willy,
From Scotland new come home?'

77A.3   ''Tis not thy father Philip,
Nor yet thy brother John;
But 'tis thy true-love, Willy,
From Scotland new come home.

77A.4   'O sweet Margret, O dear Margret,
I pray thee speak to me;
Give me my faith and troth, Margret,
As I gave it to thee.'

77A.5   'Thy faith and troth thou's never get,
Nor yet will I thee lend,
Till that thou come within my bower,
And kiss my cheek and chin.'

77A.6   'If I shoud come within thy bower,
I am no earthly man;
And shoud I kiss thy rosy lips,
Thy days will not be lang.

77A.7   'O sweet Margret, O dear Margret,
I pray thee speak to me;
Give me my faith and troth, Margret,
As I gave it to thee.'

77A.8   'Thy faith and troth thou's never get,
Nor yet will I thee lend,
Till you take me to yon kirk,
And wed me with a ring.'

77A.9   'My bones are buried in yon kirk-yard,

Afar beyond the sea,
And it is but my spirit, Margret,
That's now speaking to thee.'

77A.10 She stretchd out her lilly-white hand,
And, for to do her best,
'Hae, there's your faith and troth, Willy,
God send your soul good rest.'

77A.11 Now she has kilted her robes of green
A piece below her knee,
And a' the live-lang winter night
The dead corp followed she.

77A.12 'Is there any room at your head, Willy?
Or any room at your feet?
Or any room at your side, Willy,
Wherein that I may creep?'

77A.13 'There's no room at my head, Margret,
There's no room at my feet;
There's no room at my side, Margret,
My coffin's made so meet.'

77A.14 Then up and crew the red, red cock,
And up then crew the gray:
'Tis time, tis time, my dear Margret,
That you were going away.'

77A.15 No more the ghost to Margret said,
But, with a grievous groan,
Evanishd in a cloud of mist,
And left her all alone.

77A.16 'O stay, my only true-love, stay,'
The constant Margret cry'd;
Wan grew her cheeks, she closd her een,
Stretchd her soft limbs, and dy'd.

77C: Sweet William's Ghost

77C.1 LADY MARJORIE, Lady Marjorie,

Sat sewing her silken seam;
By her came a pale, pale ghost,
With many a sich and mane.

77C.2 'Are ye my father, the king?' she says,
'Or are ye my brother John?
Or are you my true-love, Sweet William,
From England newly come?'

77C.3 'I'm not your father, the king,' he says,
'No, no, nor your brother John;
But I'm your true love, Sweet William,
From England that's newly come.'

77C.4 'Have ye brought me any scarlets so red?
Or any silks so fine?
Or have ye brought me any precious things,
That merchants have for sale?'

77C.5 'I have not brought you any scarlets sae red,
No, no, nor the silks so fine;
But I have brought you my winding-sheet,
Oer many's the rock and hill.

77C.6 'O Lady Marjory, Lady Marjory,
For faith and charitie,
Will you give to me my faith and troth,
That I gave once to thee?'

77C.7 'O your faith and troth I'll not give thee,
No, no, that will not I,
Until I get one kiss of your ruby lips,
And in my arms you come [lye].'

77C.8 'My lips they are so bitter,' he says,
'My breath it is so strong,
If you get one kiss of my ruby lips,
Your days will not be long.

77C.9 'The cocks they are crowing, Marjory,' he says,
'The cocks they are crawing again;
It's time the deid should part the quick,

96

Marjorie, I must be gane.'

77C.10 She followed him high, she followed him low,
        Till she came to yon church-yard;
        O there the grave did open up,
        And young William he lay down.

77C.11 'What three things are these, Sweet William,' she says,
        'That stands here at your head?'
        'It's three maidens, Marjorie,' he says,
        'That I promised once to wed.'

77C.12 'What three things are these, Sweet William,' she says,
        'That stands here at your side?'
        'It is three babes, Marjorie,' he says,
        'That these three maidens had.'

77C.13 'What three things are these, Sweet William,' she says,
        'That stands here at your feet?'
        It is three hell-hounds, Marjorie,' he says,
        'That's waiting my soul to keep.'

77C.14 She took up her white, white hand,
        And she struck him in the breast,
        Saying, Have there again your faith and troth,
        And I wish your soul good rest.

77F: Sweet William's Ghost

77F.1   WHEN seven years were come and gane,
        Lady Margaret she thought lang;
        And she is up to the hichest tower,
        By the lee licht o the moon.

77F.2   She was lookin oer her castle high,
        To see what she might fa,
        And there she saw a grieved ghost,
        Comin waukin oer the wa.

77F.3   'O are ye a man of mean,' she says,
        'Seekin ony o my meat?
        Or are you a rank robber,

Come in my bower to break?'

77F.4 'O I'm Clerk Saunders, your true-love,
Behold, Margaret, and see,
And mind, for a' your meikle pride,
Sae will become of thee.'

77F.5 'Gin ye be Clerk Saunders, my true-love,
This meikle marvels me;
O wherein is your bonny arms,
That wont to embrace me?'

77F.6 'By worms they're eaten, in mools they're rotten,
Behold, Margaret, and see,
And mind, for a' your mickle pride,
Sae will become o thee.'

* * * * *

* * * * *

77F.7 'O, bonny, bonny sang the bird,
Sat on the coil o hay;
But dowie, dowie was the maid
That followd the corpse o clay.

77F.8 'Is there ony room at your head, Saunders?
Is there ony room at your feet?
Is there ony room at your twa sides,
For a lady to lie and sleep?'

77F.9 'There is nae room at my head, Margaret,
As little at my feet;
There is nae room at my twa sides,
For a lady to lie and sleep.

77F.10 'But gae hame, gae hame now, May Margaret,
Gae hame and sew your seam;
For if ye were laid in your weel made bed,
Your days will nae be lang.'

The Ojibwe Bridge to the Other Side

The Ojibwe or Chippewa (also Chippeway) are the third-largest group of Native Americans-First Nations in US and Canada, surpassed only by Cherokee and Navajo. And the Ojibwe language, which belongs to the Algonquian linguistic group, is known as *Anishinaabemowin* or *Ojibwemowin*, and is still widely spoken.

The painful lesson the youthful hunter Outalissa learns in the Chippeway tale that follows is that however strong our desire is to follow our dearly departed to the afterlife, there is a time and place for everything and there is nothing we can do to change that fact.

The Journey to the Island of Souls

Once upon a time there lived in the nation of the Chippeways a most beautiful maiden, the flower of the wilderness, the delight and wonder of all who saw her. She was called the Rock-rose, and was beloved by a youthful hunter, whose advances gained her affection. No one was like the brave Outalissa in her eyes: his deeds were the greatest, his skill was the most wonderful. It was not permitted them, however, to become the inhabitants of one lodge. Death came to the flower of the Chippeways. In the morning of her days she died, and her body was laid in the dust with the customary rites of burial. All mourned for her, but Outalissa was a changed man. No more did he find delight in the chase or on the war-path. He grew sad, shunned the society of his brethren. He stood motionless as a tree in the hour of calm, as the wave that is frozen up by the breath of the cold wind.

Joy came no more to him. He told his discontent in the ears of his people, and spoke of his determination to seek his beloved maiden. She had but removed, he said, as the birds fly away at the [Pg 130] approach of winter, and it required but due

99

diligence on his part to find her. Having prepared himself, as a hunter makes ready for a long journey, he armed himself with his war-spear and bow and arrow, and set out to the Land of Souls.

Directed by the old tradition of his fathers, he travelled south to reach that region, leaving behind him the great star. As he moved onwards, he found a more pleasant region succeeding to that in which he had lived. Daily, hourly, he remarked the change. The ice grew thinner, the air warmer, the trees taller. Birds, such as he had never seen before, sang in the bushes, and fowl of many kinds were pluming themselves in the warm sun on the shores of the lake. The gay woodpecker was tapping the hollow beech, the swallow and the martin were skimming along the level of the green vales. He heard no more the cracking of branches beneath the weight of icicles and snow, he saw no more the spirits of departed men dancing wild dances on the skirts of the northern clouds, and the farther he travelled the milder grew the skies, the longer was the period of the sun's stay upon the earth, and the softer, though less brilliant, the light of the moon.

Noting these changes as he went with a joyful heart, for they were indications of his near approach to the land of joy and delight, he came at length to a cabin situated on the brow of a steep hill in the middle of a narrow road. At the door of this cabin stood a man of a most ancient and venerable appearance. He was bent nearly double with age. His locks were white as snow. His eyes were sunk very far into his head, and the flesh was wasted from his bones, till they were like trees from which the bark has been peeled. He was clothed in a robe of white goat's skin, and a long staff supported his tottering limbs whithersoever he walked.

The Chippeway began to tell him who he was, and why he had come thither, but the aged man stopped him, telling him he knew upon what errand he was bent.

"A short while before," said he, "there passed the soul of a tender and lovely maiden, well-known to the son of the Red Elk, on her way to the beautiful island. She was fatigued with her long journey, and rested a while in this cabin. She told me the story of your love, and was persuaded that you would attempt to follow her to the Lake of Spirits."

The old man, further, told Outalissa that if he made speed he might hope to overtake the maiden on the way. Before, however, he resumed his journey he must leave behind him his body, his spear, bow, and arrows, which the old man promised to keep for him should he return. The Chippeway left his body and arms behind him, and under the direction of the old man entered upon the road to the Blissful Island. He had travelled but a couple of bowshots when it met his view, even more beautiful than his fathers had painted it.

He stood upon the brow of a hill which sloped gently down to the water of a lake which stretched as far as eye could see. Upon its banks were groves of beautiful trees of all kinds, and many canoes were to be seen gliding over its water. Afar, in the centre of the lake, lay the beautiful island appointed for the residence of the good. He walked down to the shore and entered a canoe which stood ready for him, made of a shining white stone. Seizing the paddle, he pushed off from the shore and commenced to make his way to the island. As he did so, he came to a canoe like his own, in which he found her whom he was in pursuit of. She recognised him, and the two canoes glided side by side over the water. Then Outalissa knew that he was on the Water of Judgment, the great water over which every soul must pass to reach the beautiful island, or in which it must sink to meet the punishment of the wicked. The two lovers glided on in fear, for the water seemed at times ready to swallow them, and around them they could see many canoes, which held those whose lives had been wicked, going down. The Master of Life had, however, decreed that they should pass in safety, and they reached the shores of the beautiful island, on which they landed full of joy.

It is impossible to tell the delights with which they found it filled. Mild and soft winds, clear and sweet waters, cool and refreshing shades, perpetual verdure, inexhaustible fertility, met them on all sides. Gladly would the son of the Red Elk have remained for ever with his beloved in the happy island, but the words of the Master of Life came to him in the pauses of the breeze, saying—"Go back to thy own land, hunter. Your time has not yet come. You have not yet performed the work I have for you to do, nor can you yet enjoy those pleasures which belong to them who have performed their allotted task on earth. Go back, then. In time thou shalt rejoin her, the love of whom has brought thee hither."

Despite the seeming impossibility of being reunited with those we leave behind when we depart from this life, there is always hope, for sometimes miracles do happen, at least according to the following tale:

The Funeral Fire

For several nights after the interment of a Chippewa a fire is kept burning upon the grave. This fire is lit in the evening, and carefully supplied with small sticks of dry wood, to keep up a bright but small fire. It is kept burning for several hours, generally until the usual hour of retiring to rest, and then suffered to go out. The fire is renewed for four nights, and sometimes for longer. The person who performs this pious office is generally a near relative of the deceased, or one who has been long intimate with him. The following tale is related as showing the origin of the custom:

A small war party of Chippewas encountered their enemies upon an open plain, where a severe battle was fought. Their leader was a brave and distinguished warrior, but he never acted with greater bravery, or more distinguished himself by personal prowess, than on this occasion. After turning the tide of battle against his enemies, while shouting for victory, he received an arrow in his breast, and fell upon the plain. No warrior thus killed is ever buried, and according to ancient custom, the chief was placed in a sitting posture upon the field, his back supported by a tree, and his face turned towards the direction in which his enemies had fled. His headdress and equipment were accurately adjusted as if he were living, and his bow leaned against his shoulder. In this posture his companions left him. That he was dead appeared evident to all, but a strange thing had happened. Although deprived of speech and motion, the chief heard distinctly all that was said by his friends. He heard them lament his death without having the power to contradict it, and he felt their touch as they adjusted his posture, without having the power to reciprocate it. His anguish, when he felt himself thus abandoned, was extreme, and his wish to follow his friends on their return home so completely filled his mind, as he saw them one after another take leave of him and depart, that with a terrible effort he arose and followed them. His form, however, was invisible to them, and this aroused in him surprise, disappointment, and rage, which by turns took possession of him. He followed their track, however, with great diligence. Wherever they went he went, when they walked he walked, when they ran he ran, when they encamped he stopped with them, when they slept he slept, when they awoke he awoke. In short, he mingled in all their labours and toils, but he was excluded from all their sources of refreshment, except that of sleeping, and from the pleasures of participating in their conversation, for all that he said received no notice.

"Is it possible," he cried, "that you do not see me, that you do not hear me, that you do not understand me? Will you suffer me to bleed to death without offering to stanch my wounds? Will you permit me to starve while you eat around me? Have those whom I have so often led to war so soon forgotten me? Is there no one who recollects me, or who will offer me a morsel of food in my distress?"

Thus he continued to upbraid his friends at every stage of the journey, but no one seemed to hear his words. If his voice was heard at all, it was mistaken for the rustling of the leaves in the wind.

At length the returning party reached their village, and their women and children came out, according to custom, to welcome their return and proclaim their praises.

"Kumaudjeewug! Kumaudjeewug! Kumaudjeewug! they have met, fought, and conquered!" was shouted by every mouth, and the words resounded through the most distant parts of the village. Those who had lost friends came eagerly to inquire their fate, and to know whether they had died like men. The aged father consoled himself for the loss of his son with the reflection that he had fallen manfully, and the widow half forgot her sorrow amid the praises that were uttered of the bravery of her husband. The hearts of the youths glowed with martial ardour as they heard these flattering praises, and the children joined in the shouts, of which they scarcely knew the meaning. Amidst all this uproar and bustle no one seemed conscious of the presence of the warrior-chief. He heard many inquiries made respecting his fate. He heard his companions tell how he had fought, conquered, and fallen, pierced by an arrow through his breast, and how he had been left behind among the slain on the field of battle.

"It is not true," declared the angry chief, "that I was killed and left upon the field! I am here. I live; I move; see me; touch me. I shall again raise my spear in battle, and take my place in the feast."

Nobody, however, seemed conscious of his presence, and his voice was mistaken for the whispering of the wind.

He now walked to his own lodge, and there he found his wife tearing her hair and lamenting over his fate. He endeavoured to undeceive her, but she, like the others, appeared to be insensible of his presence, and not to hear his voice. She sat in a despairing manner, with her head reclining on her hands. The chief asked her to bind up his wounds, but she made no reply. He placed his mouth close to her ear and shouted—"I am hungry, give me some food!"

The wife thought she heard a buzzing in her ear, and remarked it to one who sat by. The enraged husband now summoning all his strength, struck her a blow on the forehead. His wife raised her hand to her head, and said to her friend—"I feel a slight shooting pain in my head."

Foiled thus in every attempt to make himself known, the warrior-chief began to reflect upon what he had heard in his youth, to the effect that the spirit was sometimes permitted to leave the body and wander about. He concluded that possibly his body might have remained upon the field of battle, while his spirit only accompanied his returning friends. He determined to return to the field, although it was four days' journey away. He accordingly set out upon his way. For three days he pursued his way without meeting anything uncommon; but on the fourth, towards evening, as he came to the skirts of the battlefield, he saw a fire in the path before him. He walked to one side to avoid stepping into it, but the fire also changed its position, and was still before him. He then went in another direction, but the mysterious fire still crossed his path, and seemed to bar his entrance to the scene of the conflict. In short, whichever way he took, the fire was still before him—no expedient seemed to avail him.

"Thou demon!" he exclaimed at length, "why dost thou bar my approach to the field of battle? Knowest thou not that I am a spirit also, and that I seek again to enter my body? Dost thou presume that I shall return without effecting my object? Know that I have never been defeated by the enemies of my nation, and will not be defeated by thee!"

So saying, he made a sudden effort and jumped through the flame. No sooner had he done so than he found himself sitting on the ground, with his back supported by a tree, his bow leaning against his shoulder, all his warlike dress and arms upon his body, just as they had been left by his friends on the day of battle. Looking up he beheld a large canicu, or war eagle, sitting in the tree above his head. He immediately recognised this bird to be the same as he had once dreamt of in his youth—the one he had chosen as his guardian spirit, or personal manito. This eagle had carefully watched his body and prevented other ravenous birds from touching it.

The chief got up and stood upon his feet, but he felt himself weak and much exhausted. The blood upon his wound had stanched itself, and he now bound it up. He possessed a knowledge of such roots as have healing properties, and these he carefully sought in the woods. Having found some, he pounded some of them between stones and applied them externally. Others he chewed and swallowed. In a short time he found himself so much recovered as to be able to commence his journey, but he suffered greatly from hunger, not seeing any large animals that he might kill. However, he succeeded in killing some small birds with his bow and arrow, and these he roasted before a fire at night.

In this way he sustained himself until he came to a river that separated his wife and friends from him. He stood upon the bank and gave that peculiar whoop which is a signal of the return of a friend. The sound was immediately heard, and a canoe was despatched to bring him over, and in a short time, amidst the shouts of his friends and relations, who thronged from every side to see the arrival, the warrior-chief was landed.

When the first wild bursts of wonder and joy had subsided, and some degree of quiet had been restored to the village, he related to his people the account of his adventures. He concluded his narrative by telling them that it is pleasing to the spirit of a deceased person to have a fire built upon the grave for four nights after his burial; that it is four days' journey to the land appointed for the residence of the spirits; that in its journey thither the spirit stands in need of a fire every night at the place of its encampment; and that if the friends kindle this fire upon the spot where the body is laid, the spirit has the benefit of its light and warmth on its path, while if the friends neglect to do this, the spirit is subjected to the irksome task of making its own fire each night.

Taken from *Folk-Lore and Legends: North American Indian* by W. W. GIibbings 18 BURY ST., LONDON, W.C. 1890

Heaven Can't Wait!

Two ninety year old men, Mike and Joe, have been friends all their lives. When it's clear that Joe is dying, Mike visits him every day.

One day Mike says, 'Joe, we both loved rugby all our lives, and we played rugby on Saturdays together for so many years. Please do me one favour, when you get to Heaven, somehow you let me know if there's rugby there.'

Joe looks up at Mike from his death bed, 'Mike, you've been my best friend for many years. If it's at all possible, I'll do this favour for you.'

Shortly after that, Joe passes on. At midnight a couple of nights later, Mike is awakened from a sound sleep by a blinding flash of white light and a voice calling out to him, 'Mike-Mike.'

'Who is it? Mike asks, sitting up suddenly. 'Who is it?'

'Mike - It's me, Joe.'

'You're not Joe. Joe just died.'

'I'm telling you, it's me, Joe,' insists the voice.

'Joe! Where are you?'

'In heaven', replies Joe. 'I have some really good news and a little bad news I'm afraid.'

'Tell me the good news first,' says Mike.

'The good news,' Joe says, 'is that there is rugby in heaven. Better yet, all of our old friends who died before us are here, too. Better than that, we're all young again. Better still, it's always spring time and it never rains or snows. And best of all, we can play rugby all we want, and we never get tired.'

'That's fantastic,' says Mike. 'It's beyond my wildest dreams! So what's the bad news?'

'You're in the team for Tuesday!'

There comes a time when our voice is no longer heard, when the knowledge we have seems to count for nothing, and no one pays attention any more to what we have to say. And when we come to this point, when our life no longer seems to serve any purpose, perhaps the time is ripe to leave this world behind, and to cross over into the next one, just as Onais does in this tale.

The Sleep of One Hundred Years

It was at the time of the destruction of the First Temple. The cruel war had laid Jerusalem desolate, and terrible was the suffering of the people.

Rabbi Onias, mounted on a camel, was sorrowfully making his way toward the unhappy city. He had travelled many days and was weary from lack of sleep and faint with hunger, yet he would not touch the basket of dates he had with him, nor would he drink from the water in a leather bottle attached to the saddle.

"Perchance," he said, "I shall meet someone who needs them more than I."

But everywhere the land was deserted. One day, nearing the end of the journey, he saw a man planting a carob tree at the foot of a hill.

"The Chaldeans," said the man, "have destroyed my beautiful vineyards and all my crops, but I must sow and plant anew, so that the land may live again."

Onias passed sorrowfully on and at the top of the hill he stopped. Before him lay Jerusalem, not the once beautiful city with its hundreds of domes and minarets that caught the first rays of the sun each morning, but a vast heap of ruins and charred buildings. Onias threw himself on the ground and wept bitterly. No human being could he see, and the sun was setting over what looked like a city of the dead.

"Woe, woe," he cried. "Zion, my beautiful Zion, is no more. Can it ever rise again? Not in a hundred years can its glory be renewed."

The sun sank lower as he continued to gaze upon the ruined city, and darkness gathered over the scene. Utterly exhausted, Onias, laying his head upon his camel on the ground, fell into a deep sleep.

The silver moon shone serenely through the night and paled with the dawn, and the sun cast its bright rays on the sleeping rabbi. Darkness spread its mantle of night once more, and again the sun rose, and still Onias slept. Days passed into weeks, the weeks merged into months, and the months rolled on until years went by; but Rabbi Onias did not waken.

Seeds, blown by the winds and brought by the birds, dropped around him, took root and grew into shrubs, and soon a thick hedge surrounded him and screened him from all who passed. A date that had fallen from his basket, took root also, and in time there rose a beautiful palm tree which cast a shade over the sleeping figure.

And thus a hundred years rolled by.

Suddenly, Onias moved, stretched himself and yawned. He was awake again. He looked around confused.

"Strange," he muttered. "Did I not fall asleep on a hill overlooking Jerusalem last night? How comes it now that I am hemmed in by a thicket and am lying in the shade of this noble date palm?"

With great difficulty he rose to his feet.

"Oh, how my bones do ache!" he cried. "I must have overslept myself. And where is my camel?"

Puzzled, he put his hand to his beard. Then he gave a cry of anguish.

"What is this? My beard is snow-white and so long that it almost reaches to the ground."

He sank down again, but the mound on which he sat was but

a heap of rubbish and collapsed under his weight. Beneath it were bones. Hastily clearing away the rubbish, he saw the skeleton of a camel.

"This surely must be my camel," he said. "Can I have slept so long? The saddle-bags have rotted, too. But what is this?" and he picked up the basket of dates and the water-bottle. The dates and the water were quite fresh.

"This must be some miracle," he said. "This must be a sign for me to continue my journey. But, alas, that Jerusalem should be destroyed!"

He looked around and was more puzzled than ever. When he had fallen asleep the hill had been bare of vegetation. Now it was covered with carob trees.

"I think I remember a man planting a carob tree yesterday," he said. "But was it yesterday?"

He turned in the other direction and gave a cry of astonishment. The sun was shining on a noble city of glittering pinnacles and minarets, and around it were smiling fields and vineyards.

"Jerusalem still lives," he exclaimed. "Of a truth I have been dreaming—dreaming that it was destroyed. Praise be to God that it was but a dream."

With all speed he made his way across the plain to the city. People looked at him strangely and pointed him out to one another, and the children ran after him and called him names he did not understand. But he took no notice. Near the outskirts of the city he paused.

"Canst thou tell me, father," he said to an old man, "which is the house of Onias, the rabbi?"

"'Tis thy wit, or thy lack of it, that makes thee call me father," replied the man. "I must be but a child compared with thee."

Others gathered around and stared hard at Onias.

"Didst thou speak of Rabbi Onias?" asked one. "I know of one who says that was the name of his grandfather. I will bring him."

He hastened away and soon returned with an aged man of about eighty.

"Who art thou?" Onias asked.

"Onias is my name," was the reply. "I am called so in honour of my sainted grandfather, Rabbi Onias, who disappeared mysteriously one hundred years ago, after the destruction of the First Temple."

"A hundred years," murmured Onias. "Can I have slept so long?"

"By thy appearance, it would seem so," replied the other Onias. "The Temple has been rebuilt since then."

"Then it was not a dream," said the old man.

They led him gently indoors, but everything was strange to him. The customs, the manners, the habits of the people, their dress, their talk, was all different, and every time he spoke they laughed.

"Thou seemest like a creature from another world," they said. "Thou speakest only of the things that have long passed away."

One day he called his grandson.

"Lead me," he said, "to the place of my long sleep. Perchance I will sleep again. I am not of this world, my child. I am alone, a stranger here, and would fain leave ye."

Taking the dates and the bottle of water which still remained fresh, he made his way to where he had slept for a hundred years, and there his prayer for peace was answered. He slept again, but not in this world will he awaken.

The Milk Bride of Kadin

Bulgaria was under the yoke of the Ottoman Empire for five hundred years, and many of the Bulgarian legends are connected with that very sad phase of Bulgarian history. One of the legends is about the building of the Kadin Bridge (Kadin Most in Bulgarian) and of a great sacrifice. It is one of the most famous bridges left standing from those ancient days.

Kadin Bridge is in the village of Nevestino, near the city of Kiustendil in Southwestern Bulgaria. The bridge is made of stone and it is remarkably beautiful. There is still an inscription on it saying that it was built by the order of Vizir Ishak Pasha during the reign of Sultan Mehmed, who was also known as "The Conqueror".

The legend says that the vizir decided to build the bridge because one day, while he was on his way to Bosnia, he couldn't cross the swift-flowing waters of the river of Struma.

As the legend goes, there were three brothers who were assigned to build the bridge. So the three young men started its construction, but whatever they did, all their efforts were in vain. For whatever they managed to build during the day, the river destroyed it at night and washed everything away.

The brothers were stumped and did not know what to do. They thought long and hard about it, trying to find a solution. After many days they came to the conclusion that the river wanted something and they should offer up a sacrifice to the Struma.

In order to build the bridge and fulfill their task, the three brothers decided to build into or within the stone walls of the bridge, one of their beautiful and beloved wives. Since they could not choose which one, they decided that the first wife who brought her husband lunch the following day, should be the one to be sacrificed.

It turned out that it was the wife of the brother named Manol. Ironically, her name was Struma, just like the river.

She came first, bringing the bread she had baked for her husband and carrying in her arms their first child. The brothers, with little hesitation, took her to where they had been working. And then, stone by stone, began to build her directly into the middle of one of the vaults of the bridge.

The poor woman cried and begged for mercy, but to no avail. Finally, when she understood that the brothers would not change their minds, she made one final request to them; to leave holes in the structure for her eyes and for her breasts, so she could at least see and feed her child. Before long, though, the unfortunate mother died and her milk turned into stone on the walls of the bridge.

Since then many nursing mothers from all over Bulgaria, have come to the Milk Bridge of Kadin to scrape off tiny flakes from the stone structure. The mothers place these flakes of Kadin into boiling water to make a tea, which they then drink, in order to have enough milk for their children.

Adapted from **http://legendsguide.com/780/bulgarian-legend-the-milk-bridge-of-kadin/** [accessed 28/10/2010].

* * *

The death of those we love, as a result of wars, natural disasters, or diseases, is so very painful for those left behind as it would seem to serve no purpose and is just a waste of a life—at least as far as we, mere mortals, are able to comprehend.

In this case, however cruel the treatment of the young bride may seem to have been, it does appear to have served a purpose of sorts—a in that it not only enabled the brothers to build the bridge but it has also given hope to all those mothers with babies who now visit the site.

The Psychopomp and the Shape-Shifter

A psychopomp is a guide, whose main function is to escort souls to the afterlife. The term originates from the Greek words *pompos* (conductor or guide) and *psyche* (breath, life, soul, or mind). Examples of psychopomps include the Greek god Hermes, the Egyptian jackal-headed god Anubis, the Archangel Michael, and the female Valkyries of Teutonic legend.

In Jungian psychology, the psychopomp is a mediator between the unconscious and conscious realms, symbolically personified in dreams as a wise man or woman, or sometimes as a helpful animal. In many cultures, the shaman also fulfils the role of the psychopomp. This may include not only accompanying the soul of the dead, but also vice versa: to help at birth, to introduce the newborn child's soul to the world.

Not only are psychopomps adept at guiding others through such transformative experiences as death or other transitions, but they are often shapeshifters too, having the ability to change their appearance to match both the setting and the times they find themselves in—like the scholar in the story that follows:

The Spirit of a Buried Man

A POOR scholar was going by the highway into a town, and found under the walls of the gate the body of a dead man, unburied, trodden by the feet of the passers-by. He had not much in his purse, but willingly gave enough to bury him, that he might not be spat upon and have sticks thrown at him. He performed his devotions over the fresh heaped-up grave, and went on into the world to wander. In an oak wood sleep overpowered him, and when he awoke, he espied with wonderment a bag full of gold. He thanked the unseen beneficent hand, and came to the bank of a large river, where it was necessary to be ferried over. The two ferrymen, observing the bag full of gold, took him into the boat, and just at an eddy took from him the gold and threw him into the water. As the waves carried him away insensible, he by accident clutched a plank, and by its aid floated successfully to the shore. It was not a plank, but the spirit of the buried man, who addressed him in these words: 'You honoured my remains by burial; I thank you for it. In token of gratitude I will teach you how you can transform yourself into a crow, into a hare, and into a deer.' Then he taught him the spell. The scholar, when acquainted with the spell, could with ease transform himself into a crow, into a hare, and into a deer. He wandered far, he wandered wide, till he wandered to the court of a mighty king, where he remained as an archer in attendance at the court. This king had a beautiful daughter, but she dwelt on an inaccessible island, surrounded on all sides by the sea. She dwelt in a castle of copper, and possessed a sword such that he who brandished it could conquer the largest army. Enemies had invaded the territory of the king; he needed and desired the victorious sword. But how to obtain it, when nobody had up to that time succeeded in getting on to the lonely island? He therefore made proclamation that whoever should bring the victorious sword from the princess should obtain her hand, and, moreover, should sit upon the throne after him. No one was venturesome enough to attempt it, till the wandering scholar, then an archer attached to the court, stood before the king announcing his readiness to go, and requesting a letter, that on receipt of that token the princess might give up the weapon to him. All men were astonished, and the king entrusted him with a letter to his daughter. He went into the forest, without knowing in the least that another archer attached to the court was dogging his steps. He first transformed himself into a hare, then into a deer, and darted off with haste and speed; he traversed no small distance, till he stood on the shore of the sea. He then transformed himself into a crow, flew across the water of the sea, and didn't rest till he was on the island. He went into the castle of copper, delivered to the beautiful princess the letter from her father, and requested her to give him the victorious sword. The beautiful princess looked at the archer. He captured her heart at once. She asked inquisitively how he had been able to get to her castle, which was on all sides surrounded by water and knew no human footsteps. Thereupon the archer replied that he knew secret spells by which he could transform himself into a deer, a hare, and a crow. The beautiful princess, therefore, requested the archer to transform himself into a deer before her eyes. When he made himself into a graceful deer, and began to fawn and bound, the princess secretly pulled a tuft of fur from his back. When he transformed himself again into a hare, and bounded with pricked up ears, the princess secretly, pulled a little fur off his back. When he changed himself into a crow and began to fly about in the room, the princess secretly pulled a few feathers from the bird's wings. She immediately wrote a letter to her father and delivered up the victorious sword. The young scholar flew across the sea in the form of a crow, then ran a great distance in that of a deer, till in the neighbourhood of the wood he bounded as a hare. The treacherous archer was already there in ambush, saw when he changed himself into a hare, and recognised him at once. He drew his bow, let fly the arrow, and killed the hare. He took from him the letter and carried off the sword, went to the castle, delivered to the king the letter and the sword of victory, and demanded at once the fulfilment of the promise that had been made. The king, transported with joy, promised him immediately his daughter's hand, mounted his horse, and rode boldly against his enemies with the sword. Scarcely had he espied their standards, when he brandished the sword mightily several times, and that towards the four quarters of the world. At every wave of the sword large masses of enemies fell dead on the spot, and others, seized with panic, fled like hares. The king returned joyful with victory, and sent for his beautiful daughter, to give her to wife to the archer who brought the sword. A banquet was prepared. The musicians were already striking up, the whole castle was brilliantly lighted; but the princess sat sorrowful beside the assassin-archer. She knew at once that he was in nowise the man whom she saw in the castle on the island, but she dared not ask her father where the other handsome archer was; she only wept much and secretly: her heart beat for the other.

The poor scholar, in the hare's skin, lay slain under the oak, lay there a whole year, till one night he felt himself awakened from a mighty sleep, and before him stood the well-known spirit, whose body he had buried. He told him what had happened to him, brought him back to life, and said: 'To-morrow is the princess's wedding; hasten, therefore, to the castle without a moment's delay; she will recognise you; the archer, too, who killed you treacherously, will recognise you.' The young man sprang up promptly, went to the castle with throbbing heart, and entered the grand saloon, where numerous guests were eating and drinking. The beautiful princess recognised him at once, shrieked with joy, and fainted; and the assassin-archer, the moment he set eyes on him, turned pale and green from fear. Then the young man related the treason and murderous act of the archer, and in order to prove his words, turned himself in presence of all the assembled company into a graceful deer, and began to fawn upon the princess. She placed the tuft of fur pulled off him in the castle on the back of the deer, and the fur immediately grew into its place. Again he transformed himself into a hare, and similarly the piece of fur pulled off, which the princess had kept, grew into its place immediately on contact. All looked on in astonishment till the young man changed himself into a crow. The princess brought out the feathers which she had pulled from its wings in the castle, and the feathers immediately grew into their places. Then the old king commanded the assassin-archer to be put to death. Four horses were led out, all wild and unbroken. He was bound to them by his hands and feet, the horses were started off by the whip, and at one bound they tore the assassin-archer to pieces. The young man obtained the hand of the young and charming princess. The whole castle was in a brilliant blaze of light, they drank, they ate with mirth; and the princess did not weep, for she possessed the husband that she wished for.

The origin of this story is Polish and it was taken from *Sixty Folk-Tales from exclusively Slavonic Sources*. Translated, with Brief Introduction and Notes, BY A. H. Wratislaw. Boston: Houghton, Mifflin and Company. New York: 11, East Seventeenth Street, The Riverside Press, Cambridge. [1890] Scanned, proofed and formatted at sacred-texts.com, January, 2006, by John Bruno Hare. This text is in the public domain in the United States because it was published prior to 1923.

The Prince Who Would Seek Immortality

Once upon a time, in the very middle of the middle of a large kingdom, there was a town, and in the town a palace, and in the palace a king. This king had one son whom his father thought was wiser and cleverer than any son ever was before, and indeed his father had spared no pains to make him so. He had been very careful in choosing his tutors and governors when he was a boy, and when he became a youth he sent him to travel, so that he might see the ways of other people, and find that they were often as good as his own.

It was now a year since the prince had returned home, for his father felt that it was time that his son should learn how to rule the kingdom which would one day be his. But during his long absence the prince seemed to have changed his character altogether. From being a merry and light-hearted boy, he had grown into a gloomy and thoughtful man. The king knew of nothing that could have produced such an alteration. He vexed himself about it from morning till night, till at length an expla-nation occurred to him—the young man was in love!

Now the prince never talked about his feelings—for the matter of that he scarcely talked at all; and the father knew that if he was to come to the bottom of the prince's dismal face, he would have to begin. So one day, after dinner, he took his son by the arm and led him into another room, hung entirely with the pictures of beautiful maidens, each one more lovely than the other.

'My dear boy,' he said, 'you are very sad; perhaps after all your wanderings it is dull for you here all alone with me. It would be much better if you would marry, and I have collected here the portraits of the most beautiful women in the world of a rank equal to your own. Choose which among them you would like for a wife, and I will send an embassy to her father to ask for her hand.'

'Alas! Your Majesty,' answered the prince, 'it is not love or marriage that makes me so gloomy; but the thought, which haunts me day and night, that all men, even kings, must die. Never shall I be happy again till I have found a kingdom where death is unknown. And I have determined to give myself no rest till I have discovered the Land of Immortality.

The old king heard him with dismay; things were worse than he thought. He tried to reason with his son, and told him that during all these years he had been looking forward to his return, in order to resign his throne and its cares, which pressed so heavily upon him. But it was in vain that he talked; the prince would listen to nothing, and the following morning buckled on his sword and set forth on his journey.

He had been travelling for many days, and had left his fatherland behind him, when close to the road he came upon a huge tree, and on its topmost bough an eagle was sitting shaking the branches with all his might. This seemed so strange and so unlike an eagle, that the prince stood still with surprise, and the bird saw him and flew to the ground. The moment its feet touched the ground he changed into a king.

'Why do you look so astonished?' he asked.

'I was wondering why you shook the boughs so fiercely,' answered the prince.

'I am condemned to do this, for neither I nor any of my kindred can die till I have rooted up this great tree,' replied the king of the eagles. 'But it is now evening, and I need work no more to-day. Come to my house with me, and be my guest for the night.'

The prince accepted gratefully the eagle's invitation, for he was tired and hungry. They were received at the palace by the king's beautiful daughter, who gave orders that dinner should be laid for them at once. While they were eating, the eagle questioned his guest about his travels, and if he was wandering for pleasure's sake, or with any special aim. Then the prince told him everything, and how he could never turn back till he had discovered the Land of Immortality.

'Dear brother,' said the eagle, 'you have discovered it already, and it rejoices my heart to think that you will stay with us. Have you not just heard me say that death has no power either over myself or any of my kindred till that great tree is rooted up? It will take me six hundred years' hard work to do that; so marry my daughter and let us all live happily together here. After all, six hundred years is an eternity!'

'Ah, dear king,' replied the young man, 'your offer is very tempting! But at the end of six hundred years we should have to die, so we should be no better off! No, I must go on till I find the country where there is no death at all.'

Then the princess spoke, and tried to persuade the guest to change his mind, but he sorrowfully shook his head. At length, seeing that his resolution was firmly fixed, she took from a cabinet a little box which contained her picture, and gave it to him saying: 'As you will not stay with us, prince, accept this box, which will sometimes recall us to your memory. If you are tired of travelling before you come to the Land of Immortality, open this box and look at my picture, and you will be borne along either on earth or in the air, quick as thought, or swift as the whirlwind.'

The prince thanked her for her gift, which he placed in his tunic, and sorrowfully bade the eagle and his daughter farewell.

Never was any present in the world as useful as that little box, and many times did he bless the kind thought of the princess. One evening it had carried him to the top of a high mountain, where he saw a man with a bald head, busily engaged in digging up spadefuls of earth and throwing them in a basket. When the basket was full he took it away and returned with an empty one, which he likewise filled. The prince stood and watched him for a little, till the bald-headed man looked up and said to him: 'Dear brother, what surprises you so much?'

'I was wondering why you were filling the basket,' replied the prince.

'Oh!' replied the man, 'I am condemned to do this, for neither I nor any of my family can die till I have dug away the whole of this mountain and made it level with the plain. But, come, it is almost dark, and I shall work no longer.' And he plucked a leaf from a tree close by, and from a rough digger he was changed into a stately bald-headed king. 'Come home with me,' he added; 'you must be tired and hungry, and my daughter will have supper ready for us.' The prince accepted gladly, and they went back to the palace, where the bald-headed king's daughter, who was still more beautiful than the other princess, welcomed them at the door and led the way into a large hall and to a table covered with silver dishes. While they were eating, the bald-headed king asked the prince how he had happened to wander so far, and the young man told him all about it, and how he was seeking the Land of Immortality. 'You have found it already,' answered the king, 'for, as I said, neither I nor my family can die till I have levelled this great mountain; and that will take full eight hundred years longer. Stay here with us and marry my daughter. Eight hundred years is surely long enough to live.'

'Oh, certainly,' answered the prince; 'but, all the same, I would rather go and seek the land where there is no death at all.'

So next morning he bade them farewell, though the princess begged him to stay with all her might; and when she found that she could not persuade him she gave him as a remembrance a gold ring. This ring was still more useful than the box, because when one wished oneself at any place one was there directly, without even the trouble of flying to it through the air. The prince put it on his finger, and thanking her heartily, went his way.

He walked on for some distance, and then he recollected the ring and thought he would try if the princess had spoken truly as to its powers. 'I wish I was at the end of the world,' he said, shutting his eyes, and when he opened them he was standing in a street full of marble palaces. The men who passed him were tall and strong, and their clothes were magnificent. He stopped some of them and asked in all the twenty-seven languages he knew what the name of the city was, but no one answered him. Then his heart sank within him; what should he do in this strange place if nobody could understand anything? he said. Suddenly his eyes fell upon a man dressed after the fashion of his native country, and he ran up to him and spoke to him in his own tongue. 'What city is this, my friend?' he inquired.

'It is the capital city of the Blue Kingdom,' replied the man, 'but the king himself is dead, and his daughter is now the ruler.'

With this news the prince was satisfied, and begged his countryman to show him the way to the young queen's palace. The man led him through several streets into a large square, one side of which was occupied by a splendid building that seemed borne up on slender pillars of soft green marble. In front was a flight of steps, and on these the queen was sitting wrapped in a veil of shining silver mist, listening to the complaints of her people and dealing out justice. When the prince came up she saw directly that he was no ordinary man, and telling her chamberlain to dismiss the rest of her petitioners for that day, she signed to the prince to follow her into the palace. Luckily she had been taught his language as a child, so they had no difficulty in talking together.

The prince told all his story and how he was journeying in search of the Land of Immortality. When he had finished, the princess, who had listened attentively, rose, and taking his arm, led him to the door of another room, the floor of which was made entirely of needles, stuck so close together that there was not room for a single needle more.

'Prince,' she said, turning to him, 'you see these needles? Well, know that neither I nor any of my family can die till I have worn out these needles in sewing. It will take at least a thousand years for that. Stay here, and share my throne; a thousand years is long enough to live!'

'Certainly,' answered he; 'still, at the end of the thousand years I should have to die! No, I must find the land where there is no death.'

The queen did all she could to persuade him to stay, but as her words proved useless, at length she gave it up. Then she said to him: 'As you will not stay, take this little golden rod as a remembrance of me. It has the power to become anything you wish it to be, when you are in need.'

So the prince thanked her, and putting the rod in his pocket, went his way.

Scarcely had he left the town behind him when he came to a broad river which no man might pass, for he was standing at the end of the world, and this was the river which flowed round it. Not knowing what to do next, he walked a little distance up the bank, and there, over his head, a beautiful city was floating in the air. He longed to get to it, but how? Neither road nor bridge was anywhere to be seen, yet the city drew him upwards, and he felt that here at last was the country which he sought. Suddenly he remembered the golden rod which the mist-veiled queen had given him. With a beating heart he flung it to the ground, wishing with all his might that it should turn into a bridge, and fearing that, after all, this might prove beyond its power. But no, instead of the rod, there stood a golden ladder, leading straight up to the city of the air. He was about to enter the golden gates, when there sprang at him a wondrous beast, whose like he had never seen. 'Out sword from the sheath,' cried the prince, springing back with a cry. And the sword leapt from the scabbard and cut off some of the monster's heads, but others grew again directly, so that the prince, pale with terror, stood where he was, calling for help, and put his sword back in the sheath again.

The queen of the city heard the noise and looked from her window to see what was happening. Summoning one of her servants, she bade him go and rescue the stranger, and bring him to her. The prince thankfully obeyed her orders, and entered her presence.

The moment she looked at him, the queen also felt that he was no ordinary man, and she welcomed him graciously, and asked him what had brought him to the city. In answer the prince told all his story, and how he had travelled long and far in search of the Land of Immortality.

'You have found it,' said she, 'for I am queen over life and over death. Here you can dwell among the immortals.'

A thousand years had passed since the prince first entered the city, but they had flown so fast that the time seemed no more than six months. There had not been one instant of the thousand years that the prince was not happy till one night when he dreamed of his father and mother. Then the longing for his home came upon him with a rush, and in the morning he told the Queen of the Immortals that he must go and see his father and mother once more. The queen stared at him with amazement, and cried: 'Why, prince, are you out of your senses? It is more than eight hundred years since your father and mother died! There will not even be their dust remaining.'

'I must go all the same,' said he.

'Well, do not be in a hurry,' continued the queen, understanding that he would not be prevented. 'Wait till I make some preparations for your journey.' So she unlocked her great treasure chest, and took out two beautiful flasks, one of gold and one of silver, which she hung round his neck. Then she showed him a little trap-door in one corner of the room, and said: 'Fill the silver flask with this water, which is below the trap-door. It is enchanted, and whoever you sprinkle with the water will become a dead man at once, even if he had lived a thousand years. The golden flask you must fill with the water here,' she added,

pointing to a well in another corner. 'It spring
eternity; you have only to sprinkle a few drops o\e rock of
will come to life again, if it had been a thousand ye\y and it

The prince thanked the queen for her gifts, and, bi\d.'
farewell, went on his journey.

He soon arrived in the town where the mist-veiled qu
reigned in her palace, but the whole city had changed, and he
could scarcely find his way through the streets. In the palace
itself all was still, and he wandered through the rooms without
meeting anyone to stop him. At last he entered the queen's own
chamber, and there she lay, with her embroidery still in her
hands, fast asleep. He pulled at her dress, but she did not waken.
Then a dreadful idea came over him, and he ran to the chamber
where the needles had been kept, but it was quite empty. The
queen had broken the last over the work she held in her hand,
and with it the spell was broken too, and she lay dead.

Quick as thought the prince pulled out the golden flask, and
sprinkled some drops of the water over the queen. In a moment
she moved gently, and raising her head, opened her eyes.

'Oh, my dear friend, I am so glad you wakened me; I must
have slept a long while!'

'You would have slept till eternity,' answered the prince, 'if I
had not been here to waken you.'

At these words the queen remembered about the needles. She
knew now that she had been dead, and that the prince had
restored her to life. She gave him thanks from her heart for what
he had done, and vowed she would repay him if she ever got a
chance.

The prince took his leave, and set out for the country of the
bald-headed king. As he drew near the place he saw that the
whole mountain had been dug away, and that the king was lying
dead on the ground, his spade and bucket beside him. But as
soon as the water from the golden flask touched him he yawned
and stretched himself, and slowly rose to his feet. 'Oh, my dear

glad to see you,' cried he, 'I must have slept a long

friend,

while ould have slept till eternity if I had not been here to

you,' answered the prince. And the king remembered the

we ntain, and the spell, and vowed to repay the service if he ever

d a chance.

Further along the road which led to his old home the prince found the great tree torn up by its roots, and the king of the eagles sitting dead on the ground, with his wings outspread as if for flight. A flutter ran through the feathers as the drops of water fell on them, and the eagle lifted his beak from the ground and said: 'Oh, how long I must have slept! How can I thank you for having awakened me, my dear, good friend!'

'You would have slept till eternity if I had not been here to waken you'; answered the prince. Then the king remembered about the tree, and knew that he had been dead, and promised, if ever he had the chance, to repay what the prince had done for him.

At last he reached the capital of his father's kingdom, but on reaching the place where the royal palace had stood, instead of the marble galleries where he used to play, there lay a great sulphur lake, its blue flames darting into the air. How was he to find his father and mother, and bring them back to life, if they were lying at the bottom of that horrible water? He turned away sadly and wandered back into the streets, hardly knowing where he was going; when a voice behind him cried: 'Stop, prince, I have caught you at last! It is a thousand years since I first began to seek you.' And there beside him stood the old, white-bearded, figure of Death. Swiftly he drew the ring from his finger, and the king of the eagles, the bald-headed king, and the mist-veiled queen, hastened to his rescue. In an instant they had seized upon Death and held him tight, till the prince should have time to reach the Land of Immortality. But they did not know how quickly Death could fly, and the prince had only one foot across the border, when he felt the other grasped from behind, and the voice of Death calling: 'Halt! Now you are mine.'

The Queen of the Immortals was watching from her window, and cried to Death that he had no power in her kingdom, and that he must seek his prey elsewhere.

'Quite true,' answered Death; 'but his foot is in my kingdom, and that belongs to me!'

'At any rate half of him is mine,' replied the Queen, 'and what good can the other half do you? Half a man is no use, either to you or to me! But this once I will allow you to cross into my kingdom, and we will decide by a wager whose he is.'

And so it was settled. Death stepped across the narrow line that surrounds the Land of Immortality, and the queen proposed the wager which was to decide the prince's fate. 'I will throw him up into the sky,' she said, 'right to the back of the morning star, and if he falls down into this city, then he is mine. But if he should fall outside the walls, he shall belong to you.'

In the middle of the city was a great open square, and here the queen wished the wager to take place. When all was ready, she put her foot under the foot of the prince and swung him into the air. Up, up, he went, high amongst the stars, and no man's eyes could follow him. Had she thrown him up straight? The queen wondered anxiously, for, if not, he would fall outside the walls, and she would lose him forever. The moments seemed long while she and Death stood gazing up into the air, waiting to know whose prize the prince would be. Suddenly they both caught sight of a tiny speck no bigger than a wasp, right up in the blue. Was he coming straight? No! Yes! But as he was nearing the city, a light wind sprang up, and swayed him in the direction of the wall. Another second and he would have fallen half over it, when the queen sprang forward, seized him in her arms, and flung him into the castle. Then she commanded her servants to cast Death out of the city, which they did, with such hard blows that he never dared to show his face again in the Land of

Immortality.

This story, translated from *Ungarischen Volksmurchen*, was taken from *The Crimson Fairy Book* (1903) edited by Andrew Lang, one of a twelve-book series of fairy tales compiled by him. As acknowledged in the prefaces, although Lang himself made most of the selections, his wife and other translators did a large portion of the translating and telling of the actual stories. So the irony of Lang's life and work is that although he wrote for a profession, he is remembered for the works he did *not* write.

From being a merry and light-hearted boy, *The Prince Who Would Seek Immortality* grew into a gloomy and thoughtful man, all caused by focusing on the future instead of the here and now. There are many traditional stories of this type, based on the search for everlasting life, from the Japanese tale of *Urashima Taro* (see Berman, 2008) to the Georgian story *The Earth will take its Own* (see Berman, 2007), but a happy ending is an exception. So although, like more or less everyone, you might not have all that you would like to have, at least make sure you learn to appreciate what it is you do have in this life to be thankful for.

References

Berman, M. (2007) *The Nature of Shamanism and the Shamanic Story*, Newcastle: Cambridge Scholars Publishing.

Berman, M. (2008) *Soul Loss and the Shamanic Story*, Newcastle: Cambridge Scholars Publishing.

A ticket to Suleti? – Not yet please!

For many people, coming back from a Near Death Experience, results in them turning to God, a god, a guardian angel, a spirit helper, or an inner guide in gratitude for the new lease of life they have been given. But whoever those of us who have survived a NDE may turn to, one thing is for sure—that an experience of such magnitude leads us to reassess our former lifestyles and to hopefully make changes for the better. Unfortunately, memories inevitably fade, though, and in time we can forget what we learnt in the process of our "rebirth", which is why some of us need another shock to the system at some later date to remind us of what really matters in life.

The Old Man and Death:

An old labourer, bent double with age and years of hard work, was gathering firewood in a forest. At last he grew so tired and hopeless that he threw down the bundle he had managed to collect, and cried out in pain: "I can't bear this life any longer. I just wish Death would come, take me, and put an end to all this suffering!"

As he spoke, Death, a grisly skeleton, appeared and said to him: "What can I do for you Mortal? I heard you calling me."

"Please, sir," replied the woodcutter, "I wonder if you'd mind helping me to lift this bundle on to my shoulder so I can continue on my way once more?"

So in future be careful what you wish for, or else it could well come true!

In the Caucasus, in the Republic of Georgia, the Bedis Mtserlebi were one or several deities that recorded and decided human fate; similar to the Greek moiras or Roman parcae/fatae. They lived in Suleti or the world of dead souls, and constantly consulted the Book of Fates (bedis tsigni). They supervised every human life and notified the god of the dead (suletis ghmerti) when a person's lifetime was over. Special heralds (mgrebrebi) were then sent to take the soul of the person whose time was up and conduct it to the underworld.

* * *

In the Republic of Georgia, the story is told of a grandson and his grandfather. The boy asks his grandfather how many more years he will live, and the old man answers "I will live as long as you will." The boy, surprised by the answer, asks how that can be possible, to which the grandfather replies: "I will live as long as you will remember me."

According to the Georgian tradition, there are special days during the year, especially at Easter time, to remember all those people who are in the other world. The bridge between the two worlds is said to be very narrow and you will be there before you know it – it takes just a moment. The Georgian word *tsutisopeli* is used to describe this life, best translated as "a one minute world." So we need to be sure we make the most of it!

The Mother's Malison

In this ballad, Willie, against his mother's advice, goes to May Margaret's home, where he is not admitted. He then drowns in the Clyde. May Margaret wakes and says she dreamed of him. Her mother tells her that he had been there half an hour before, and she goes after him.

A malison is an archaic word for a curse, and one way to counter such a curse would have been to consult a charmer.

Charming was a distinct tradition, based on either the possession of an innate healing touch, ownership of a healing object, or most commonly the possession of one or more simple verse charms usually based on extracts from the New Testament or apocryphal biblical stories. .. In many areas charms could only remain efficacious if they were transmitted to someone of the opposite sex. ... The charms were concerned with a well-defined range of natural ailments ... There was no ambiguity about what charmers did ... They were merely custodians of a God-given gift, not masters of equivocal magical forces (Davies, 2007, p.83).

Charms could be produced for a variety of purposes, such as the detection of thieves and the procurement of love, but the majority were concerned with the protection of humans and livestock from witchcraft and the curing of those already bewitched. Magical texts usually specified that such charms had to be written on either virgin or unborn parchment. The former was made from the skin of an animal that had not yet reached sexual maturity, while the latter was made from unborn animals that were either cut out of the uterus or aborted (ibid. p.147). Most written charms contained a strong religious element ... Scriptural passages were often reproduced in Latin, with the occasional smattering of Greek or Hebrew. Such passages were often badly spelt and grammatically poor, presumably from repeated copying. Not surprisingly, there was also considerable use of overtly magical words and phrases, spirit names, occult symbols, planetary signs, and astrological terms. If a charm was intended to protect a human, the cunning-person would often conceal it in a little bag with the injunction that it be kept close to the body and should never be allowed to touch the ground. To avoid this fate, charms were sewn into clothing, worn around the neck or tucked into corsets (ibid. p.148).

What is evident from all this is that "magic did a lot of the work later taken over by pharmaceutical medicine, fertilizers, insurance schemes and advertisement columns" (Hutton, 1993, p.290), and those practising more than likely "saw charms and rituals in the same functional sense as these modern commodities and services" (ibid. p.290). Most practitioners of the art would have had just one or two stock charms that they reproduced over and over again, personalising them by adding the client's name. In the case of Willie, we have no way of knowing whether he consulted a charmer or not, but if he did it certainly did not help him.

"Sceptics will argue that it is impossible to eliminate from analysis the Christian influence on what sources there are available to us, such that we can never be certain in any one case that we are indeed dealing with beliefs that are authentically pagan. This view is now so widely held that we can in justice think of it as the prevailing orthodoxy" (Winterbourne, 2007, p.24).

Jewett was aware of this problem too, as the following quote shows:

The superstition that pervades European folklore is sometimes curiously interwrought with Christianity and sometimes frankly pagan. The unschooled imagination turns constantly to the supernatural to account for the mysterious, the unexplained, and readily finds in mere sequence of incidents relations of cause and effect. A mother in anger curses her child, and the child, departing from home, is overtaken by fatal disaster. The inference is plain. It is the mother's malison (Child, No. 216) that brings Sweet Willie to his death in the roaring Clyde; it is the mother's curse that makes the little bride unable to hold fast to her lover at the perilous ford (Jewett, 1913, p.15).

"The old religions of these islands perished a very long time ago, and absolutely. They fell before Christianity both because of tricks of fortune and because they were not well equipped to resist the new faith" (Hutton, 1993, p.341). And what we have left is rather like a jigsaw puzzle from which most of the pieces are missing. Nevertheless, just because a task is difficult, in this case eliminating from analysis the Christian influence on what sources there are available to us, is no reason for us not to attempt to do so. If it was, then no progress would ever be made in any research that we might be involved in.

Ballads of death for love are not ... always tragic nor even truly pathetic, but run all along from the fateful to the inconsequent and absurd, more than once strongly suggesting parody. Though the man of the ballads is frequently both faithful and heroic, it is the woman to whom most often love is a thing to live and to die for. There are coquettes among the ballad women, but they are fewer than the faithful maidens and wives. The typical woman of the ballads ... waits for her lover, follows him, dies of longing for him, or takes her own life when she has lost him (Jewett, 1913, p.4).

In *The Mother's Malison*, it is the last course of action that the woman takes, death by drowning, to be reunited with her true love in the next life:

216C: The Mother's Malison, or, Clyde's Water
216C.1   WILLIE stands in his stable-door,
        And clapping at his steed,

And looking oer his white fingers
His nose began to bleed.

216C.2   'Gie corn to my horse, mother,
And meat to my young man,
And I'll awa to Maggie's bower;
I'll win ere she lie down.'

216C.3   'O bide this night wi me, Willie,
O bide this night wi me;
The best an cock o a' the reest
At your supper shall be.'

216C.4   'A' your cocks, and a' your reests,
I value not a prin,
For I'll awa to Meggie's bower;
I'll win ere she lie down.'

216C.5   'Stay this night wi me, Willie,
O stay this night wi me;
The best an sheep in a' the flock
At your supper shall be.'

216C.6   'A' your sheep, and a' your flocks,
I value not a prin,
For I'll awa' to Meggie's bower;
I'll win ere she lie down.'

216C.7   'O an ye gang to Meggie's bower,
Sae sair against my will,
The deepest pot in Clyde's water,
My malison ye's feel.'

216C.8   'The guid steed that I ride upon
Cost me thrice thretty pound;
And I'll put trust in his swift feet
To hae me safe to land.'

216C.9   As he rade ower yon high, high hill,
And down yon dowie den,
The noise that was in Clyde's water
Woud feard five huner men.

216C.10 'O roaring Clyde, ye roar ower loud,
Your streams seem wondrous strang;
Make me your wreck as I come back,
But spare me as I gang!'

216C.11 Then he is on to Maggie's bower,
And tirled at the pin;
'O sleep ye, wake ye, Meggie,' he said,
'Ye'll open, lat me come in.'

216C.12 'O wha is this at my bower-door,
That calls me by my name?'
'It is your first love, sweet Willie,
This night newly come hame.'

216C.13 'I hae few lovers thereout, thereout,
As few hae I therein;
The best an love that ever I had
Was here jusr late yestreen.'

216C.14 'The warstan stable in a' your stables,
For my puir steed to stand!
The warstan bower in a' your bowers,
For me to lie therin!
My boots are fu o Clyde's water,
I'm shivering at the chin.'

216C.15 'My barns are fu o corn, Willie,
My stables are fu o hay;
My bowers are fu o gentlemen,
They'll nae remove till day.'

216C.16 'O fare ye well, my fause Meggie,
O farewell, and adieu!
I've gotten my mither's malison
This night coming to you.'

216C.17 As he rode ower yon high, high hill,
And down yon dowie den,
The rushing that was in Clyde's water
Took Willie's cane frae him.

216C.18 He leand him ower his saddle-bow,
To catch his cane again;
The rushing that was in Clyde's water
Took Willie's hat frae him.

216C.19 He leand him ower his saddle-bow,
To catch his hat thro force;
The rushing that was in Clyde's water
Took Willie frae his horse.

216C.20 His brither stood upo the bank,
Says, Fye, man, will ye drown?
Ye'll turn ye to your high horse head
And learn how to sowm.

216C.21 'How can I turn to my horse head
And learn how to sowm?
I've gotten my mither's malison,
It's here that I maun drown.'

216C.22 The very hour this young man sank
Into the pot sae deep,
Up it wakend his love Meggie
Out o her drowsy sleep.

216C.23 'Come here, come here, my mither dear,
And read this dreary dream;
I dreamd my love was at our gates,
And nane wad let him in.'

216C.24 'Lye still, lye still now, my Meggie,
Lye still and tak your rest;
Sin your true-love was at your yates,
It's but twa quarters past.'

216C.25 Nimbly, nimbly raise she up,
And nimbly pat she on,
And the higher that the lady cried,
The louder blew the win.

216C.26 The first an step that she steppd in,
She stepped to the queet;

'Ohon, alas!' said that lady,
'This water's wondrous deep.'

216C.27   The next an step that she wade in,
She wadit to the knee;
Says she, 'I coud wide farther in,
If I my love coud see.'

216C.28   The next an step that she wade in,
She wadit to the chin;
The deepest pot in Clyde's water
She got sweet Willie in.

216C.29   'You've had a cruel mither, Willie,
And I have had anither;
But we shall sleep in Clyde's water
Like sister an like brither.'

References

Child, F.J. (1886-98) *The English and Scottish Popular Ballads*, Boston, New York, Houghton, Mifflin and Company. Ballads originally transcribed by Cathy Lynn Preston. HTML Formatting at sacred-texts.com. This text is in the public domain. These files may be used for any non-commercial purpose, provided this notice of attribution is left intact.

Davies, O. (2007) *Popular Magic: Cunning-folk in English History*, London & New York: Hambledon Continuum.

Hutton, R. (1993) *The Pagan Religions of the Ancient British Isles: Their Nature and Legacy*, Oxford: Blackwell Publishing.

Jewett, S. (trans.) (1913) *Folk-Ballads of Southern Europe*, translated into English Verse by Sophie Jewett. New York and London: G. P. Putnam's Sons. http://www.archive.org/details/folkballadsofsouOOjewe

Winterbourne, A. (2007) *When The Norns Have Spoken: Time and Fate in Germanic Paganism*, Wales: Superscript.

The Devil's Bridge, Austria

Almost every country possesses some legend of a "Devil's Bridge," and how the Evil One has been ultimately cheated by his own handiwork, and the Tyrol, which is alive with legends and superstitions, is not behind any other in this respect. What is of particular interesting about the story that follows, though, is that it succeeds in killing two birds with one stone, as it also explains why goats have no tails, more or less.

In the valley of Montafon, the bridge of the village broke down, or rather the swollen torrent carried it away; and as the parish was anxious to restore it as soon as possible, the villagers of course being unable to pass to and from Schruns, on the other side of the river, for all their daily wants, they applied to the village carpenter, and offered him a large sum of money if he would rebuild the bridge in three days' time. This puzzled the poor fellow beyond description; he had a large family and now his fortune would be made at once; but he saw the impossibility of finishing the work in so short a time, and therefore he begged one day for reflection.

Then he set to work to study all day, up to midnight, to find out how he could manage to do the work within the specified time; and as he could find out nothing, he thumped the table with his fist, and called out, "To the devil with it! I can find out nothing."

In his anger and annoyance he was on the point of going to bed, when all at once a little man wearing a green hat entered the room, and asked, "Carpenter, wherefore so sad?" and then the carpenter told him all his troubles.

The little fellow replied, "It is very easy to help you. I will build your bridge, and in three days it shall be finished, but only on the condition that the first soul out of your house who passes over the bridge shall be mine."

On hearing this, the carpenter, who then knew with whom he had to do, shuddered with horror, though the large sum of money enticed him, and he thought to himself, "After all, I will cheat the devil," and so he agreed to the contract.

Three days afterwards the bridge was complete, and the devil stood in the middle, awaiting his prey. After having remained there for many days, the carpenter at last appeared himself, and at that sight the devil jumped with joy; but the carpenter was driving one of his goats, and as he approached the bridge, he pushed her on before him, and called out, "There you have the first soul out of my house," and the devil seized upon the goat.

But, oh, grief and shame! First disappointed, and then enraged, he dragged the poor goat so hard by her tail that it came out, and then off he flew, laughed at and mocked by all who saw him.

Since that time it is that goats have such short tails.

Source: Marie Alker Günther, *Tales and Legends of the Tyrol* (London: Chapman and Hall, 1874), pp. 179-81.

Leesom Brand

Just occasionally, there are journeys back from the other side, and an account of one such occasion is described in this Scottish ballad, one of the less well-known ones.

There could well be a shamanic past behind *Beowulf* and other Old English poems and early poetry could well be an art form rooted in tribal tradition that therefore retains traces of native beliefs. "Too many reflexes occur in the literature for us to ignore the influential role shamanism played in Anglo-Saxon prehistory" (Glosecki, 1989, p.3), and how it went on to influence later poetry / ballads too. In this chapter both the shamanic and Christian themes to be found in *Leesom Brand*, Child Ballad 15, will be explored.

As is the case with a number of ballads, what we find in *Leesom Brand* is an interesting mix of both pagan and Christian references in the text. First of all, however, before looking at these, what follows is a synopsis of the story.

When just ten years old, Leesom Brand goes into service in what seems to be a foreign or unknown land. An eleven-year-old girl falls in love with him there, but nine months later calls on him to saddle two horses, take her dowry, and flee with her. They head to his mother's house, but the girl goes into labour on the way. He then goes off to hunt, but violates a prohibition she lays on him, either not to hunt a milk-white hind, or to come running when called and, as a result, she and his son die. Heartbroken, he returns home and tells his mother all about it. Some variants stop at this point. In others, the mother gives him a horn with ointment that restores the girl and the infant to life.

And here are the lyrics in their entirety:

Leesom Brand

15A.1 MY boy was scarcely ten years auld,
Whan he went to an unco land,
Where wind never blew, nor cocks ever crew,
Ohon for my son, Leesome Brand!

15A.2 Awa to that king's court he went,
It was to serve for meat an fee;
Gude red gowd it was his hire,
And lang in that king's court stayd he.

15A.3 He hadna been in that unco land
But only twallmonths twa or three,
Till by the glancing o his ee,
He gaind the love o a gay ladye.

15A.4 This ladye was scarce eleven years auld,
When on her love she was right bauld;
She was scarce up to my right knee,
When oft in bed wi men I'm tauld.

15A.5 But when nine months were come and gane,
This ladye's face turnd pale and wane.

15A.6 To Leesome Brand she then did say,
'In this place I can nae mair stay.

15A.7 'Ye do you to my father's stable,
Where steeds do stand baith wight and able.

15A.8 'Strike ane o them upo the back,
The swiftest will gie his head a wap.

15A.9 'Ye take him out upo the green,
And get him saddled and bridled seen.

15A.10 'Get ane for you, anither for me,horses vehicles
And lat us ride out ower the lee.

15A.11 'Ye do you to my mother's coffer,
And out of it ye'll take my tocher.

15A.12 'Therein are sixty thousand pounds,
Which all to me by right belongs.'

15A.13 He's done him to her father's stable,

Where steeds stood baith wicht and able.

15A.14   Then he strake ane upon the back,
The swiftest gae his head a wap.

15A.15   He's taen him out upo the green,
And got him saddled and bridled seen.

15A.16   Ane for him, and another for her,
To carry them baith wi might and virr.

15A.17   He's done him to her mother's coffer,
And there he's taen his love's tocher;

15A.18   Wherein were sixty thousand pound,
Which all to her by right belongd.

15A.19   When they had ridden about six mile,
His true love then began to fail.

15A.20   'O wae's me,' said that gay ladye,
'I fear my back will gang in three!

15A.21   'O gin I had but a gude midwife,
Here this day to save my life,

15A.22   'And ease me o my misery,
O dear, how happy I would be!'

15A.23   'My love, we're far frae ony town,
There is nae midwife to be foun.

15A.24   'But if ye'll be content wi me,
I'll do for you what man can dee.'

15A.25   'For no, for no, this maunna be,'
Wi a sigh, replied this gay ladye.

15A.26   'When I endure my grief and pain,
My companie ye maun refrain.

15A.27   'Ye'll take your arrow and your bow,
And ye will hunt the deer and roe.

15A.28   'Be sure ye touch not the white hynde,
For she is o the woman kind.'

15A.29   He took sic pleasure in deer and roe,
Till he forgot his gay ladye.

15A.30   Till by it came that milk-white hynde,

And then he mind on his ladye syne.

15A.31   He hasted him to yon greenwood tree,
For to relieve his gay ladye;

15A.32   But found his ladye lying dead,
Likeways her young son at her head.

15A.33   His mother lay ower her castle wa,
And she beheld baith dale and down;
And she beheld young Leesome Brand,
As he came riding to the town.

15A.34   'Get minstrels for to play,' she said,
'And dancers to dance in my room;
For here comes my son, Leesome Brand,
And he comes merrilie to the town.'

15A.35   'Seek nae minstrels to play, mother,
Nor dancers to dance in your room;
But tho your son comes, Leesome Brand,
Yet he comes sorry to the town.

15A.36   'O I hae lost my gowden knife;
I rather had lost my ain sweet life!

15A.37   'And I hae lost a better thing,
The gilded sheath that it was in.'

15A.38   'Are there nae gowdsmiths here in Fife,
Can make to you anither knife?

15A.39   'Are there nae sheath-makers in the land,
Can make a sheath to Leesome Brand?'

15A.40   'There are nae gowdsmiths here in Fife,
Can make me sic a gowden knife;

15A.41   'Nor nae sheath-makers in the land,
Can make to me a sheath again.

15A.42   'There ne'er was man in Scotland born,
Ordaind to be so much forlorn.

15A.43   'I've lost my ladye I lovd sae dear,
Likeways the son she did me bear.'

15A.44   'Put in your hand at my bed head,

> There ye'll find a gude grey horn;
> In it three draps o' Saint Paul's ain blude,
> That hae been there sin he was born.

15A.45
> 'Drap twa o them o your ladye,
> And ane upo your little young son;
> Then as lively they will be
> As the first night ye brought them hame.'

15A.46
> He put his hand at her bed head,
> And there he found a gude grey horn,
> Wi three draps o' Saint Paul's ain blude,
> That had been there sin he was born.

15A.47
> Then he drappd twa on his ladye,
> And ane o them on his young son,
> And now they do as lively be,
> As the first day he brought them hame.

The style of storytelling most frequently employed in both shamanic stories and in fairy tales is that of magic realism, in which although "the point of departure is 'realistic' (recognizable events in chronological succession, everyday atmosphere, verisimilitude, characters with more or less predictable psychological reactions), … soon strange discontinuities or gaps appear in the 'normal,' true-to-life texture of the narrative" (Calinescu, 1978, p.386). In other words, what happens is that our expectations based on our intuitive knowledge of physics are ultimately breached and knocked out. It is also the style of storytelling we can find employed in ballads. In *Leesom Brand*, for example, verisimilitude is established by providing us with the ages of the key figures and exactly where and when they met: The boy 'was scarcely ten years auld', the girl was 'scarce eleven years auld' and their relationship started 'But only twallmonths twa or three' after the boy started working in the king's court.

That the boy and the girl flee together on horseback in the ballad can be explained by the fact that it was probably the most frequently used form of transport at the time, but it should also be noted that the horse is also frequently the form of transport used by the shaman to access other worlds.

Pre-eminently the funerary animal and psychopomp, the "horse" is employed by the shaman, in various contexts, as a means of achieving ecstasy, that is, the "coming out of oneself" that makes the mystical journey possible. ... The "horse" enables the shaman to fly through the air, to reach the heavens. ... The horse carries the deceased into the beyond; it produces the "break-through in plane," the passage from this world to other worlds (Eliade, 1964, p.467).

The shamanic journey frequently involves passing through some kind of gateway. As Eliade explains:

The "clashing of rocks," the "dancing reeds," the gates in the shape of jaws, the "two razor-edged restless mountains," the "two clashing icebergs," the "active door," the "revolving barrier," the door made of the two halves of the eagle's beak, and many more—all these are images used in myths and sagas to suggest the insurmountable difficulties of passage to the Other World [and sometimes the passage back too] (Eliade, 2003, pp.64-65).

This gateway takes the boy 'to an unco land, Where wind never blew, nor cocks ever crew' As for the journey home, the boy is issued with strict instructions to ensure it passes without anything untoward happening:

15A.26   'When I endure my grief and pain,
        My companie ye maun refrain.

15A.27   'Ye'll take your arrow and your bow,
        And ye will hunt the deer and roe.

15A.28   'Be sure ye touch not the white hynde,
        For she is o the woman kind.'

The white hind would appear to be the equivalent of a Spirit

Helper, sent to provide support and protection to the couple, but by killing it, the boy opens them to attack.

Writing or talking about shamanism has always been problematic as "the subject area resists 'objective' analysis and is sufficiently beyond mainstream research to foil ...writing [or talking] about it in a conventional academic way" (Wallis, 2003, p.13).

Shamans have their own ways of describing trance experience. Outsiders might call them 'metaphors', but to shamans these metaphors, such as 'death', are real, lived experiences ... 'Metaphor is a problematic term extracted from Western literary discourse which does not do justice to non-Western, non-literary shamanic experiences. In recognising this limitation, 'metaphor may remain a useful term for explaining alien shamanic experiences in terms understandable to Westerners (Wallis, 2003, p.116).

Perhaps this is why the accounts of memorable shamanic journeys were often turned into folktales or ballads, as it was the only way to make them both understandable and acceptable to people not familiar with the landscapes to be found and experiences to be had in such worlds.

As for the Christian reference, the three drops of St Paul's blood to revive the dead, this more than likely stems from the life-bestowing powers of the blood of Christ, and the belief by the naïve and unsuspecting in miraculous cures and holy relics that were sold to them in the Middle Ages by the unscrupulous.

We can read of the life-giving powers of the blood of Christ in JOHN 6:53-55: Then Jesus said unto them, Verily, verily, I say unto you, Except ye eat the flesh of the Son of man, and drink his blood, ye have no life in you. Whoso eateth my flesh, and drinketh my blood, hath eternal life; and I will raise him up at the last day. For my flesh is meat indeed, and my blood is drink indeed.

However, this Christian reference could well be later addition to a much older pagan ballad as examples of the restorative powers of blood abound from earlier times, and traditional religions such as Christianity inherited their attitude towards blood and animal sacrifice from pagan origins. For example:

Closely related to Zoroastrianism, Mithraism was the religion which brought richer ideals of blood sacrifice to Judaism as it mutated, via Paul, into Christianity [Crabtree 2002]. And in the Persian holy texts, the Avesta, it is said that a Messiah will appear at the end of time and bring the triumph of good over evil and make a potion of immortality for mankind from the fat of a great bull mixed with Hamoa juice. The bull is seen as a symbol of spring, of rebirth, and a very common carving is of Mithras cleansing himself in the blood of a bull. Ritual killing of bulls and washing in its blood was believed to be necessary for cleansing, eternal life and salvation. This was followed by a meal of the bulls flesh. Life anew could be created from the flesh and blood of the sacrificed bull. http://www.humanreligions.info/animal _slaughter.html

The Mysteries of Mithras, like Christianity, celebrated these sacrificial rites symbolically rather than literally, and an icon of Mithras slaying a bull was used as an altar-piece, rather than enacting the actual sacrifice.

In the mythology of Ancient Greece, the Gorgons were three powerful, winged daemons named Medousa (Medusa), Sthenno and Euryale. Of the three sisters only Medousa was mortal, and so it was her head which King Polydektes of Seriphos commanded the young hero Perseus to fetch. He accomplished this with the help of the gods who equipped him with a reflective shield, curved sword, winged boots and helm of invisibility. When he fell upon Medousa and decapitated her, two creatures sprang forth from the wound - the winged horse Pegasus and the giant Khrysaor. And from this stems the belief that her blood had life-giving powers. We can read about the death of Medusa and the birth of Pegasus in Hesiod's Theogony, the Greek epic from the 8th or 7th B.C.

And we learn from Bibliotheca 2. 144 by the Greek mythographer Pseudo-Apollodorus, that Asclepius became so skilled in his profession as a surgeon that he not only saved lives but even revived the dead. This was because he had received from Athene the blood that had coursed through the Gorgo's veins. He used the left-side portion to destroy people, but the blood from the right side he used for their preservation, which is how he could revive those who had died.

Chapter 21, Section 4 of the 1922 version of *The Golden Bough* by Sir James George Frazer examines the widely held pagan belief that the soul is in the blood, and that therefore any ground on which it may fall necessarily becomes taboo or sacred. And the whole of chapter 47 Section 3 consists of various accounts of human sacrifices of blood to ensure the success of the crops, which pre-date Christianity too.

There are also Wiccan fertility spells using drops of blood, freely available on the Internet, such as the following:

Spell of Design of a Child: During their fertile period to hold three candles in a triangle. At the top should be silver (the Moon), left, a brown (earth) and right, blue (water). These are the symbols of the Mother. Take a rose (flower only) and place the center of the triangle. Using a thorn on the rose stem, prick your finger and squeeze three drops of blood on top of flowering. Repeat the following: "Sweet as the rose in May and be as strong as the backbone of the union of flesh and spirit, my daughter was born" Show a rose bush grow and bloom earlier. The flowers smell good and bones are evidence that the woman is both beautiful and powerful. Soft solids. Keep that image in your mind for a few minutes. Imagine the rustle of leaves in the wind, the drift of butterflies around flowers. Now, imagine a baby lying in the depths of the forest, gently swaying in the stems and buds of curling. Picture how you want your daughter to be happy, healthy, smiling. Keep this picture for a moment. When ready, take the rose and place it under the mattress before making love. Let the candles burn. Every night, before trying to conceive, repeat the use of candles and rose again to flourish. Keep in mind, this spell increases the likelihood of conceiving the sex you want. This means you cannot conceive at all if the potential child was of the opposite sex! So think long and hard about using this spell. http://www.spells-magic.com/wiccan-fertility-spells .html

So animal sacrifice and the use of blood has been a traditional element of religions since ancient times, and the fact that the ballad in its present form refers to the blood of St Paul should in no way lead us to believe that was always the case.

As to why it should be precisely three drops of blood, two for the mother and one for the baby, three has long been regarded as a magic number. It is linked with the phases of the moon (waxing, full and waning), and with time (past, present and future). Pythagoras called three the perfect number in that it represented the beginning, the middle and the end, and he thus regarded it as a symbol of Deity. The use of the number in the ballad could well be the result of the influence of Christianity and its use of the Trinity, but it also refers to the three stages in the cycle of life and adds to the universality of the story's appeal.

"Sceptics will argue that it is impossible to eliminate from analysis the Christian influence on what sources there are available to us, such that we can never be certain in any one case that we are indeed dealing with beliefs that are authentically pagan. This view is now so widely held that we can in justice think of it as the prevailing orthodoxy" (Winterbourne, 2007, p.24).

And the same argument could be applied to the attempt to ascertain whether we are dealing with beliefs that are authentically shamanic in *Leesom Brand*. Nevertheless, just because a task is difficult is no reason for not attempting it. If it was, then no progress would ever be made in any research that we might be involved in.

References

Calinescu, M. (1978) 'The Disguises of Miracle: Notes on Mircea Eliade's Fiction.' In Bryan Rennie (ed.) (2006) *Mircea Eliade: A Critical Reader*, London: Equinox Publishing Ltd.

Child, F.J. (1886-98) *The English and Scottish Popular Ballads*, Boston, New York, Houghton, Mifflin and Company. Ballads originally transcribed by Cathy Lynn Preston. HTML Formatting at sacred-texts.com. This text is in the public domain. These files may be used for any non-commercial purpose, provided this notice of attribution is left intact.

'Animal Sacrifice and Blood Rituals in Traditional World Religions and Satanism' by Vexen Crabtree 2008 http://www.humanreligions.info/animal_slaughter.html

Eliade, M. (1964) *Myth and Reality*, London: George Allen & Unwin

Eliade, M. (2003) *Rites and Symbols of Initiation*, Putnam, Connecticut: Spring Publications (originally published by Harper Bros., New York, 1958).

Frazer, J. G. (1922) *The Golden Bough: A Study in Magic and Religion*, New York: Macmillan.

Glosecki, S.O. (1989) *Shamanism and Old English Poetry*, New York: Garland Publishing Inc.

Wallis, Robert J. (2003) *Shamans/Neo-Shamans: Ecstasy, Alternative Archaeologies and Contemporary Pagans*, London: Routledge.

Winterbourne, A. (2007) *When The Norns Have Spoken: Time and Fate in Germanic Paganism*, Wales: Superscript.

Standing on the Bridge

One of the poet Henry Wadsworth Longfellow's favourite metaphors is the backward glance, by means of which people in the present look back into their distant pasts to make a discovery which provides them with a newfound source of strength. In the poem that follows, the fact that the river was, is, and will always be is a comfort to the poet and helps him to place the suffering he has had to endure within a broader context, thus enabling him to better come to terms with it.

The Bridge

I stood on the bridge at midnight,
As the clocks were striking the hour,
And the moon rose o'er the city,
Behind the dark church-tower.

I saw her bright reflection
In the waters under me,
Like a golden goblet falling
And sinking into the sea.

And far in the hazy distance
Of that lovely night in June,
The blaze of the flaming furnace
Gleamed redder than the moon.

Among the long, black rafters
The wavering shadows lay,
And the current that came from the ocean
Seemed to lift and bear them away;

As, sweeping and eddying through them,
Rose the belated tide,
And, streaming into the moonlight,
The seaweed floated wide.

And like those waters rushing
Among the wooden piers,
A flood of thoughts came o'er me
That filled my eyes with tears.

How often, oh, how often,
In the days that had gone by,
I had stood on that bridge at midnight
And gazed on that wave and sky!

How often, oh, how often,
I had wished that the ebbing tide
Would bear me away on its bosom
O'er the ocean wild and wide!

For my heart was hot and restless,
And my life was full of care,
And the burden laid upon me
Seemed greater than I could bear.

But now it has fallen from me,
It is buried in the sea;
And only the sorrow of others
Throws its shadow over me.

Yet whenever I cross the river
On its bridge with wooden piers,
Like the odor of brine from the ocean
Comes the thought of other years.

And I think how many thousands
Of care-encumbered men,
Each bearing his burden of sorrow,
Have crossed the bridge since then.

I see the long procession
Still passing to and fro,
The young heart hot and restless,
And the old subdued and slow!

And forever and forever,
As long as the river flows,
As long as the heart has passions,
As long as life has woes;

The moon and its broken reflection
And its shadows shall appear,
As the symbol of love in heaven,
And its wavering image here.
Henry Wadsworth Longfellow

William Wordsworth found standing on a bridge overlooking a river, in his case the Thames, an uplifting and life-affirming experience too:

Composed Upon Westminster Bridge
Earth has not anything to show more fair:
Dull would he be of soul who could pass by
A sight so touching in its majesty:
This City now doth like a garment wear
The beauty of the morning; silent , bare,
Ships, towers, domes, theatres, and temples lie
Open unto the fields, and to the sky,
All bright and glittering in the smokeless air.

Never did the sun more beautifully steep
In his first splendour, valley, rock, or hill;
Ne'er saw I, never felt a calm so deep!
The river glideth at his own sweet will:
Dear God! the very houses seem asleep;
And all that mighty heart is lying still!
William Wordsworth

So the next time life gets on top of you, as it invariably will, try standing on a bridge yourself. Alternatively, the sea might be what you need to provide you with the source of strength you seek:

All that holds you back
Remember
When the strength you once had at your fingertips
Fails you
And your energy seems to be spent
You too can tap into the source of power we are all part of
The very same power that drives the waves onto the beach
And then draws them out to sea again.
All that holds you back is you yourself

The Spring of Eternal Life

The Waters have been described as the reservoir of all the potentialities of existence because they not only precede every form but they also serve to sustain every creation. Immersion is equivalent to dissolution of form, in other words death, whereas emergence repeats the cosmogonic act of formal manifestation, in other words re-birth (see Eliade, 1952, p.151). And, following on from this, the surface of water can be defined as "the meeting place and doorway from one realm to another: from that which is revealed to that which is hidden, from conscious to unconscious" (Shaw & Francis, 2008, p.13).

The idea of regeneration through water can be found in numerous pan-cultural tales about the miraculous Fountain of Youth, and water can be seen to be both purifying and regenerative. So pervasive were these legends that in the 16th century the Spanish conquistador Ponce de Leon actually set out to find it once and for all—and found Florida instead.

The folktale that follows is all about the Spring of Eternal Life and comes from Ossetia in the Caucasus. It was translated by Ketevan Kalandadze. The Spring of Eternal Life, in that it represents a way back from the Other Side, enables us to bring the journey undertaken in this book full circle.

A Poor Man and a Snake

There was a poor man who had nothing except his wife, a daughter and a son. He had no land, no cattle, absolutely nothing, so there was no way he could provide for his family at all. He has to send his son to be a shepherd and work for a rich neighbour, his daughter was employed looking after their home, and he and his wife worked as a servants.

His wife was washing laundry, cleaning wheat, spinning wool, sewing and knitting and, as a reward for all this, all she was getting was a mart* (approximately 4 kg) of wheat. The man was cutting the grass for the rich neighbour's cattle, bringing back wood from the forest, and was ploughing this nobleman's land, and this is how they managed to survive.

One day during harvest he took his sickle and went to the field. He worked very hard but at the end of the day his owner put just two marts* of wheat for him in a sack as payment for two months' work. Nevertheless, the poor man took the sack and went home happy. When he crossed the field though, he noticed that the katchatchebi (a type of bush) were on fire, and that a snake was crawling toward its hole in the ground but would clearly be unable to make it in time, before the flames engulfed him too. So it crawled on to a bush, but then that bush caught fire too.

When the poor man approached the bush, the snake begged him for help: "Traveller, for sake of your blessed parents, save me from burning, and I will be of use to you. Help me by providing me with a stick I can crawl down."

The poor man didn't hesitate. He immediately held his stick out, the snake rolled on to it, and was saved by then wrapping itself around the poor man's neck.

"If you're giving me a reward, please give it to me now and then we can each go our separate ways," said the man.

"You are asking me for a reward? Are you crazy! I'm first going to strangle you and then to eat you," replied the snake. "But if you find someone who can tell us that they have ever met or heard about a snake being thankful, I promise I'll let you go. If you can't though, then you will surely die."

"Let someone else judge then please."

The snake agreed. They decided to listen to three opinions before making a decision. What could the poor man do? He had no choice but to accept the situation and just hope for the best. He was walking with the snake wrapped around his neck. Who knows if they were walking a little while or lot, but they saw a traveller. The poor man told him his story and asked him his opinion, or at least to teach him how to get rid of the snake.

"Well I've travelled a lot," the traveller replied, "but I have to admit I've never seen or heard any snake replying kindly to kindness. So I'm afraid I really can't help you."

"So his opinion proved to be of no help to you" said the snake. "And it looks as if I'm going to get my way after all."

Shortly afterwards they met a bear along the way, and the poor man asked him the same question.

"My ancestors and I have always been regarded as consultants by all the other animals because of our vast knowledge, but even I have never come across such a case—never in my lifetime have I heard of any snake responding with kindness to kindness. Try asking someone else," was the only answer the bear could come up with.

At this point, the poor man got so scared that his knees started to shake. But luckily he saw a lion coming towards them, and decided to tell him all about his problem.

The lion roared loudly, and this is what he said: "If you both have a complaint and want me to be the judge, then both of you should stand in front of me. As you know, judging is normally done that way. Then you can each tell me your side of the story. And I'm afraid that's only way I can pass any judgement. So you put your rucksack down on the ground and stand over there," said the lion to the man, "and you too, come down and stand next to him," he said to the snake.

So the poor man put his rucksack down and the snake slithered down on to the ground too.

The lion roared at the man once again, even more loudly this time: "Nobody should ever have mercy on those who don't value kindness and do wrong instead. So my judgement is this: Use your sword, hanging on your belt and cut the snake's head off."

On hearing this, the snake frantically tried to climb up on to the man again but the man quickly took his sword and cut the snake into two.

"Now use a stone to beat the bottom half of the snake," continued the lion "and, with the stick, throw it away as far as you can. Then bury it exactly there where it lands. The top half of the snake, with its head, will crawl to the Spring of Eternal Life, bring water back from there and, if it manages to wet its other half, the snake will grow seven times longer then it was before. So wait and watch until it comes back and make sure you crush the head with a stone, for if you don't do that, it won't die."

The head part of the snake reached the Spring of Eternal Life, just as the lion had said it would, held water in its mouth and came back to look for its bottom half, but of course it wasn't there. In anger, it started to lash out at the stones that had been used to bury it. But the man did as the lion had told him, took one of the stones and used it to crush the snake's head.

"You see, you were lucky to meet me," the lion spoke again, "otherwise what would have happened to you? You must have been crazy to think you could trust a snake!"

"Don't worry - I've learnt my lesson this time," the poor man replied, and I'm not going to be cheated by anyone ever again.

"Come with me and I will teach you where the Spring of Eternal Life is. It might make your life easier in future. But, whatever you see there, try not to be afraid."

The lion walked in front and the man followed him. They crossed the field and got to the foot of a mountain. A bare cliff rose in front of them and it blocked their way. The man was gobsmacked but the lion found a narrow entrance and squeezed in through it. The man followed his example, and they came upon the entrance to a cave. There they found a dragon seated on a nest of eggs, waiting for them to hatch.

The dragon got angry on seeing the lion and the man, and opened its enormous mouth ready to swallow them alive. But at that exact moment the lion bit its neck and dug out the dragon's eyes. The dragon tried to catch hold of them but couldn't see a thing. The man helped the lion and together they killed the dragon. They also destroyed all its eggs.

It turned out that this dragon was the guardian the Spring of Eternal Life. In the roof of the dragon's cave the lion and the poor man saw a skylight, from where water was gushing down. And this was the Spring of Eternal Life they had come in search of.

The lion and the man washed their faces in the spring; the man took some water with him too and they started the journey back home again.

When they came to a safe place, they said good-bye to each other and went in different directions from there on.

The man went home to his family with his sack. It so happened though, that at the same time, all the king's messengers were out and about, delivering the message that the king's only son had been fatally wounded, and that the king was prepared to give half of his kingdom and his eternal gratitude to anyone who could save him!

Although the poor man had barely stepped through his doorway when he heard the news, he immediately packed a small bag, took his water with him, and set off to see the king. He arrived at the king's palace on the following day. He gave the king's son water and he became seven times more handsome, seven times more powerful and also seven times healthier than he had been before.

The king was over the moon and held an enormous feast to celebrate the miraculous recovery of his beloved son. However, let's be honest. Which king gives half of his kingdom to a poor man? None! But he did give the poor man oxen and three sacks of wheat. Better than nothing.

The poor man returned home happy. He still had to work hard to provide for his family, but ever since then one thing has changed—he has never made the mistake of trusting a snake again.

* * *

The Ossetians are "the distant descendants and last representatives of the northern Iranians whom the ancients called Scythians and Sarmatians and who, at the dawn of the Middle Ages, under the name of the Alani and Roxolani, made Europe quake with fear" (Bonnefoy, 1993, p.262).

The ancestors of the Ossetians were the Alans, and the Daryal Gorge takes its name from them ("Dar-i-Alan", Gate of the Alans). They wandered as nomads over the steppes watered by the Terek, Kuban and Don Rivers until the Huns, under Attila, swept into Europe and split them into two parts. One group of the Alans moved into Western Europe; along with another wandering people, the Vandals, they passed through Spain into North Africa, where they disappear from history (Pearce, 1954, p.12). The other group were forced southwards and eventually settled along the Terek, immediately north of the main Caucasus Range. There they entered into trading and cultural relations with other people of the Black Sea region, and in the tenth century were converted to Christianity.

Polytheism is characteristic of the world of beliefs of nomads, and the Samartian Alans were no exception to this. Batraz was the Alan god of war, and there was also a mother goddess who was the equivalent of the Greek Potnia Theron. As for the cult of the Sun and the Moon, beside altars dated from the end of the 6th and the beginning of the 5th centuries BC, smoking vessels have been found. It is highly likely that the people who took part in the rituals would have been overcome by the smoke produced from these vessels, and that this could have resulted in them entering altered states of consciousness, which is of course what shamans frequently did (see Vaday, 2002, pp.215-221).

The dissolution of the Soviet Union posed particular problems for the Ossetian people, who were divided between North Ossetia, which was part of the Russian SFSR, and South Ossetia, part of the Georgian SSR. In December 1990 the Supreme Soviet of Georgia abolished the autonomous Ossetian enclave amid the rising ethnic tensions in the region, and much of the population fled across the border to North Ossetia or Georgia proper.

So the Ossetes today are a divided people, with one group (Kudakhtsy) living in South Ossetia (Georgia) and the majority living in North Ossetia (Russia). The latter are comprised of two ethnic sub-groups, Irontsy and Digortsy, each of them possessing their own dialect. North Ossetia ... was renamed 'North Ossetia-Alania' in 1994 with an aspiration to drop 'North Ossetia' at some stage, so that remaining 'Alania' would include both the South and the North (Matveena, 1999, p.89).

However, in the summer of 2008, everything changed. For on 7 August, after a series of low-level clashes in the region, Georgia tried to retake South Ossetia by force. Russia launched a counterattack and the Georgian troops were ousted from both South Ossetia and Abkhazia. This was followed by Russia recognising the independence of the two breakaway regions. The rest of the world, however, has not followed suit, and what the future will bring remains uncertain at this point.

References

Berman, M. (2010) *Shamanic Journeys through the Caucasus*, Hampshire: O Books (for the background information on Ossetia).

Bonnefoy, Y. (comp.) (1993). *American, African and Old European Mythologies*. Chicago and London, The University of Chicago Press.

Eliade, M. (1991) Images and Symbols, New Jersey: Princeton University Press (The original edition is copyright Librairie Gallimard 1952).

Matveena, A. (1999). *The North Caucasus: Russia's Fragile Borderland*. London: The Royal Institute of International Affairs.

Pearce, B. (1954). "The Ossetians In History." In Rothstein, A. (Ed.) (1954), *A People Reborn: The Story of North Ossetia*, 12-17. London: Lawrence & Wishart.

Shaw, S. & Francis, A. (eds.) (2008) *Deep Blue: Critical reflections on Nature, Religion and Water*, London: Equinox Publishing Ltd.

Vaday, A. (2002). "The World of Beliefs of the Sarmatians." A Nograd Megyei Muzeumok Evkonyve XXVI.

From predominantly traditional tales and ballads about creating a bridge to the other side to very much a contemporary one, but one that links both the old and the new together:

Daniel's Last Wish

Daniel wasn't stupid and realised he was going downhill fast, with probably little time left. It was a faulty heart valve coupled with a prolapsed disc in his back—each problem adversely impacting on the other and leaving him virtually bedbound. As for the option of an operation to replace the valve, it was deemed too risky given his age and generally precarious state of health.

It was therefore a time for settling unfinished business, for making plans for what would follow and Daniel had one last wish—to renew his wedding vows with the woman he loved as their original wedding day had unfortunately been one to forget rather than remember. Most of it had been spent with them queuing up for an appointment in the Home Office in Croydon, trying to sort out his wife's status in the UK, leading to frayed tempers on both sides by the time they eventually reached the Registry Office for the nothing but business like ceremony.

Beach weddings in some exotic location such as the Caribbean were by this stage out of the question, with Daniel being unable to walk more than ten paces without having to pause to catch his breath, so something closer to home and more manageable needed to be considered instead, and it was while doing some research for one final book he was planning to write that he came upon a solution to the problem: The Stone of Odin in the Orkney Islands. And this is what he found written about it:

A young man had seduced a girl under promise of marriage, and she proving with child, was deserted by him: The young man was called before session; the elders were particularly severe. Being asked by the minister the cause of so much rigour, they answered, "You do not know what a bad man this is; he has broken the promise of Odin."

Being further asked what they meant by the promise of Odin, they put him in mind of the stone at Stenhouse, on the island of Pomona, with the round hole in it; and added, that it was customary, when promises were made, for the contracting parties to join hands through this hole, and the promises so made were called the promises of Odin.

It was said that a child passed through the hole when young would never shake with palsy in old age. Up to the time of its destruction, it was customary to leave some offering on visiting the stone, such as a piece of bread, or cheese, or a rag, or even a stone.

Unfortunately, he did not read to the end of the account, though, for if he had, he would have discovered the stone no longer existed:

The Odin stone, long the favourite trysting-place in summer twilights of Orkney lovers, was demolished in 1814 by a sacrilegious farmer, who used its material to assist him in the erection of a cow house. This misguided man was a Ferry-Louper (the name formerly given to strangers from the south), and his wanton destruction of the consecrated stone stirred so strongly the resentment of the peasantry in the district that various unsuccessful attempts were made to burn his house and holdings about his ears.

However, what Daniel did manage to discover was that:

Upon the first day of every New Year the common people, from all parts of the country, used to meet at the Kirk of Stainhouse (Stennis), each person having provision for four or five days; they continued there for that time dancing and feasting in the kirk.

This meeting gave the young people an opportunity of seeing each other, which seldom failed in making four or five marriages every year; and to secure each other's love, till an opportunity of celebrating their nuptials, they had resource to the following solemn engagements:

The parties agreed stole from the rest of their companions, and went to the Temple of the Moon, where the woman, in presence of the man, fell down on her knees and prayed the god Wodden (for such was the name of the god they addressed upon this occasion) that he would enable her to perform all the promises and obligations she had and was to make to the young man present, after which they both went to the Temple of the Sun, where the man prayed in like manner before the woman, then they repaired from this to the stone [known as Wodden's or Odin's Stone], and the man being on one side and the woman on the other, they took hold of each other's right hand through the hole, and there swore to be constant and faithful to each other.

This ceremony was held so very sacred in those times that the person who dared to break the engagement made here was counted infamous, and excluded all society.

The "Temple of the Moon" is a circle of standing stones also known as the "Ring of Stennis" and the "Temple of the Sun" is a circle of standing stones also known as the "Ring of Brogar." [Source: County Folk-Lore, vol. 3: Examples of Printed Folk-Lore Concerning the Orkney & Shetland Islands, collected by G. F. Black and edited by Northcote W. Thomas (London: Folk-Lore Society, 1903).]

With the impulsiveness which had always been part of his nature, he immediately set about planning a trip to the islands, as he felt this would be the ideal place for what he had in mind. And as he wanted it all to be a surprise, he wouldn't tell his partner why but gave her the money to have her hair done and to buy a special outfit, and asked her to fix the necessary time off work for the special occasion. .

Due to the, by then, extremely tenuous state of his health, everything had to be planned down to the last detail, especially the travel and accommodation arrangements, all accomplished over the Internet from his bed with great secrecy. A Magical Mystery Tour is what he called it, and to stop her from having any inkling of where they would be going, he told her to take her passport with her for the trip. By the time they eventually reached the destination, what little energy he had left was long since exhausted. His wife, realising how tired he was, made him go straight to bed, where he quickly fell asleep. Before he did so, though, he said something strange to her, something she was never to forget:

"Although we met late in life and I was never able to do some of the things with you that I had been able to do when I was younger, I want you to know that you were the only partner I was ever faithful to, despite all the suspicions you had of me earlier in our relationship."

"Don't worry about that now, you silly old sausage, it's time to sleep—you've got a long day ahead of you tomorrow" was her answer. And these were the last words they were ever to say to each other because Daniel then closed his eyes, never to open them again.

Fortunately, she had the support of a large circle of friends who arranged for the transfer of the coffin back to London, where he had made arrangements to be buried in a plot by the side of his parents. Unlike her, never being the most sociable of persons, Daniel had only a very small circle of friends, and they barely filled the hall where the prayers were conducted prior to the procession to the grave. As for the special outfit Daniel had given her money to buy for the renewal of their vows, although its colourful nature caused the rabbi to raise his eyebrows and the more conservative family members to show their disapproval too, she defiantly wore it to the funeral service as she knew such "a poke in the eye" to the establishment would have pleased him a lot. And that was her gift to him.

An Afterthought

A writer died and was given the option of going to heaven or hell.

She decided to check out each place first. As the writer descended into the fiery pits, she saw row upon row of writers chained to their desks in a steaming sweatshop. As they worked, they were repeatedly whipped with thorny lashes.

"Oh my," said the writer. "Let me see heaven now."

A few moments later, as she ascended into heaven, she saw rows of writers, chained to their desks in a steaming sweatshop. As they worked, they, too, were whipped with thorny lashes.

"Wait a minute," said the writer. "This is just as bad as hell!"

"Oh no, it's not," replied an unseen voice. "Here, your work gets published."

Moon Books, invites you to begin or deepen your encounter with Paganism, in all its rich, creative, flourishing forms.